I0687373

COLORADO TAKEDOWN

THE MCALLISTER BROTHERS BOOK ONE

CRICKET ROHMAN

COLORADO TAKEDOWN

Cricket Rohman

This is a work of fiction. Names, characters, places, and incidents are the product of the author's imagination or are used fictitiously. Any resemblance to actual persons, living or dead, business establishments, events, or locales is entirely coincidental.

Cover design & interior formatting by:
Sweet 'N Spicy Designs

ISBN: 978-0-9994819-5-0
Ebook ISBN: 978-0-9994819-4-3

NOVELS BY CRICKET ROHMAN

Saving Madeline

Standalone Contemporary Fiction

The McAllister Brothers Series

Romantic Western Adventures

Colorado Takedown

Montana Countdown

Wyoming Sundown

The Creative Hearts Sweet Romance Series

Creative Women Novellas

Phoebe's Photo Fetish

Anna's Animal House

Caitlin's Cow Wash

Tina's Tasty Tours

The Lindsey Lark Series

Fiction with Elements of Romance & Mystery

Wanted: An Honest Man

Letters, Lovers, & Lies

Hit The Road, Jake!

The Fantasy Maker Series

Contemporary Adventures

Forever Island

Winter's Blush

ACKNOWLEDGMENTS

I would like to say thank you to:

My excellent and talented feedback readers: Jerry Gallegos, Robert Ruesch, Georgia Brousseau, Amir Bavar, and Debra Greenacre.

Author, Richard D. Rowland for his positive, encouraging thoughts about horses, life, and miracles.

Author, Danni Rose. She was the first person to read my initial manuscript. After receiving her helpful edits and content comments, I returned to my laptop for some serious revision.

My final (editing) line of defense: Bonny Milne, who finds the little things the rest of us missed.

Steve M. Tackett for his kind, uplifting words when I needed them, and for setting me straight about lanterns, propane, and real cowboys.

For Charlie,
My red-speckled heeler.
Run with Joy
Rest In Peace

THE CITY GAL, THE COWBOY, & THE ACCIDENT

ONE

Rick slammed on the brakes, spun the Range Rover around, and headed in the opposite direction—the wrong direction. Caught off balance by his sudden recklessness, Hannah's bare feet slid off the dashboard, and her leg slammed into the car's door. Her heart pounded and adrenaline raced through her body.

Before she could voice a single, recognizable word, Rick veered off the highway, slowed down, and rolled gently into the parking area of a quaint little chapel. There a dozen or so guests tossed handfuls of rice toward a smiling bride and groom.

Hannah rubbed her knee and turned down the thumping hip-hop music blaring from the radio. "What are you doing, and why are we stopping here?"

"You'll see." He was up to something. But then, he always was.

"We have two hours of driving ahead of us, and you know I want to get to the ranch before dark," Hannah said, glaring at him.

He flashed a grin her way. "Come on! Let's do it."

"Do what?"

"Get married."

"Huh?" Tipping her head, Hannah's pretty green eyes peered over the top of her sunglasses. "You're kidding, right?"

"Hey, it's me. Would I kid?"

He was exasperating but could always make her laugh even when she didn't want to. "You're crazy, and you know that was never part of our plan," she said, wagging a judgmental finger at him.

"Wait here." All smiles, he jumped out of the car and headed toward the chapel's front steps, strutting with confidence.

The last few wedding goers lingered as Rick rushed up, grasped the preacher's outstretched hand, and started talking. Before long, he glanced back at Hannah, conveying another grin, this one loaded with mischief. What was he up to now?

A surge of discomfort bubbled up in Hannah's chest.

The joke had gone a little too far this time. He'd been teasing her about getting married for several months, but lately, he'd campaigned for her hand with marked persistence. It had been funny, almost flattering at first, but now his silliness had surpassed the brink of annoying.

He turned and loped back to her, his expression sheepish.

"Sorry, babe, no wedding for us today. The guy said we'd need a Colorado marriage license. Imagine that. But he also said he'd be happy to perform a fake wedding ceremony if we were interested." His head nodded as if that might get Hannah to go along with his foolish idea.

"Oh, really? A 'fake' ceremony? Doesn't sound like preacher talk to me," she said, arching an eyebrow and grinning at his silly persistence.

"Maybe not those exact words, but—"

Hannah liked Rick. He was the only real friend she'd ever had. But marriage? No! She wasn't in love, and marriage was not even at the bottom of her lengthy to-do list. She was not about to let anything sabotage their upcoming adventure or her personal goals for future happiness.

They drove on in comfortable silence. With the music turned off, the purr of the engine lulled Hannah into a light sleep until the unfamiliar sound of gravel crunching beneath their tires prompted her eyes to open. She bolted upright, looking everywhere at once. "Are we here? Is *this* our ranch?"

Mesmerized by the magnificent greenery visible in all directions—nothing like the dry desert she'd left behind —Hannah held her breath, waiting for their new home, the ranch house they would share, to come into view. When it appeared, the sight was dreamlike and almost too good to be true. Compared with the cramped apartments she lived in most of her life, this ranch house, though obviously old, was as grand as a mansion.

Hannah leaped from the SUV before it came to a complete stop and dashed toward her first real home. A home that would bear her name, not some landlord's name.

"Slow down, Hannah."

"No way! Why don't you hurry up?" she called out without glancing back.

He caught up with her just as she reached the top of the steps. Then, to her surprise, he scooped her into his arms and stepped toward the threshold.

Nearly nose-to-nose, she managed to say, "I think a few rules accompany such an action."

"Since when did you become an avid rule follower?"

"Just now."

They laughed, and he dropped a light kiss on her forehead. "You ready?"

"More than ready. Let's go."

Their Great Adventure was about to begin.

TWO

Rick leaned against the door, awkwardly digging in his pocket for the house key, but to his surprise, the door creaked open. He exhaled with relief, thankful that he didn't need to locate the key right then, and carried Hannah inside. Almost immediately, she pulled away from his grasp and, with her feet firmly on the floor, shook her head in disbelief.

"Oh, no." Her eyes locked onto the shocking scene surrounding them and her nose wrinkled at the musty odor. While what she'd seen of the land was truly magnificent, and the exterior of the house seemed to be in good repair, the interior was in dire need of – everything. Rick hardly seemed to notice the mess and showed no concern whatsoever.

"I'm going to take a look around outside," he said. "Be right back."

Hannah peered through one of the many dirty windows, barely illuminating the kitchen and living room areas, watching him circle the house, then head to the corral. He glanced up now and then to give her a wave and a gleeful smile. She'd never seen him so excited. Not even on the day he told her the good news.

He'd located a ranch for them in Colorado. Said it was the perfect place for him to live out his cowboy fantasy, and where she could take the time to figure out what would bring her lasting happiness. All Hannah knew for sure? It was time to move on from her unsatisfying city, party-girl life.

Hannah's attention returned to the bleak, neglected interior. Space was not an issue; she knew the ranch house had ample square footage. But every inch of it was coated with dirt and dust thicker than the soles on her new, sparkling flip-flops. A thorough cleaning would be the first step—though a baby step—on this long staircase of unexpected chores.

I can do this. It'll be fun.

She hadn't planned on the adventure beginning with so many domestic tasks. The job before her was daunting, and a mental shopping list soon monopolized her thoughts. For inspiration, country living and ranch house magazines rose to the top of that list. A list that would be lengthy by the time they drove back to town for supplies. The drive would be lengthy too.

There was nothing between the ranch and the nearest town except a winding, two-lane mountain road edged with pine trees, meadows, cliffs, and boulders. No Dairy Queen, no Circle K, nothing. The seclusion of this ranch house threatened to take her breath away. Still, she managed to smile.

So this is what it's like to be a country girl.

Hannah made several trips back to the Range Rover to fetch the suitcase, backpack, and the few small boxes containing her drawing supplies and personal mementos. It didn't take long. She hadn't brought much. Leaving reminders of her old life behind added to the excitement of this promising, new beginning. As she set the last box down, Rick bounded up the front steps two at a time, clutching a bottle of wine in one hand and a corkscrew in the other.

"Grab some glasses, babe. I'm about to make a toast to the first day of our ranch life."

She cringed whenever he called her 'babe' and gave him a teasing glare, then searched the cupboards in vain for two glasses.

"Sorry. No glasses, no cups, no mugs."

"No problem," he said, lifting the bottle into the air,

his eyes shining. "To the good life. To my dream-come-true life. To the ranch life."

Rick took a swig from the bottle, wiped his mouth with the back of his hand, and passed it to her. "Your turn."

"Hmm. To never, ever again, wonder if I'll have enough money to pay my rent." She swallowed, sighed, then passed the bottle back.

"I'll drink to that." Rick's smile was contagious.

Swallow number two flowed smoothly down their throats. So did number three. Pausing, Hannah mused out loud that a bell pepper and mushroom pizza would go oh-so-nicely with the oaky, fruity merlot.

"Your wish is my command. I noticed a pizza place when we drove through Stillwater."

"You don't need to do that. Stillwater is a forty-five-minute drive from here."

Rick shrugged. "I don't mind. I'm hungry too. Want to come?"

Her mouth watered, and her stomach growled for a pizza, but the rest of her could not face the long drive. "No, I'll wait here and see what I can accomplish while you're gone. I want to begin cleaning up this place. I'm not willing to sleep on this much dust and dirt.

Rick shrugged, gave her a silly salute, and headed out to the car.

Hannah cracked open a grimy window to infuse the house with a little fresh air and found herself captivated by the view of the lower pasture to the north. The land nestled comfortably between two pine-covered hills, forming a vast ocean of green. Dusk crept in unnoticed, and the green hills faded to gray. Hannah realized she'd lost track of time and had accomplished nothing. Rick would be back in less than an hour.

She left the vanishing view and went in search of the bedrooms. Knowing this was a furnished, four-bedroom ranch house, she hoped to find at least two beds each in a separate room. She found only one, and that presented a problem. She and Rick had never slept in the same apartment before, let alone in the same bed. Rick would have no trouble with the bed shortage, but Hannah wanted no part of that. She'd sleep on the tattered old loveseat in the living room if necessary.

The sun disappeared below the western hills, and the gray of dusk quickly became the darkness of night. If she were going to explore the rooms, the closets, and all the other nooks and crannies while waiting for Rick to return, she'd need more light.

She flipped the nearest switch. Nothing happened. She tried another, then another. None of the lights worked. Odd. They all contained light bulbs; she'd checked. They couldn't all have burnt out at the same time, could they? She unscrewed one and shook it. The expected, faint rattling sound of a burnt-out bulb wasn't there.

Before the creeping feeling of anxiety had completed its journey from her head down to her toes, the problem became clear. No electricity. So much for Rick taking care of *everything* like he'd promised. And he should have been back by now. He was long overdue. Darn. She couldn't call him. She'd left her cell phone in the Range Rover's console. Then she remembered he liked his independence and, when it came to his whereabouts, he rarely checked in. She was certain he'd show up any minute.

Even so, with no electricity, no cell phone, and no neighbors that she knew of, disturbing second thoughts crept in. *What have I gotten myself into?* This mountain ranch was a far cry from her Phoenix apartment. Twinges of fear soon advanced to flashes of panic. The total darkness, the blackness – not even a street light off in the distance – brought unwanted thoughts of lurking danger.

She curled up on the dusty leather loveseat and covered herself with the only available blanket. Was there a logical reason for Rick's lateness? Maybe he had a flat tire, or something blocked the only road that led to the ranch. Could he have gotten lost? The drive was rather long and curvy, but it required making only one turn off Main Street. No! Getting lost made no sense. Perhaps he drank a beer while waiting for the pizza, and that one beer turned into many. He did like his beer.

The last of the wine did little to soothe her nerves. She lay alone in the quiet, deepening darkness, and though she feared she might not be able to sleep, she dozed off. One nonsensical dream delighted her sleeping mind with mystical horses winging their way across the tops of pine trees. They smiled. They whinnied and beckoned her to join them.

Her dream-self was about to follow the flying herd when suddenly she woke up. For a split-second, Hannah was completely lost in the inky shadows, her mind and thoughts disoriented. She blinked hard and forced her eyes open wide, but there was nothing to see except darkness. Her fingers dug into the arms of the loveseat, and she remembered where she was.

Exhaling with slight relief, Hannah glanced at her watch and found its tiny bit of light oddly soothing. However, the time itself was not. It was 2:12 in the morning. Rick should have found his way back to the ranch long before now.

Hannah shivered, nervous sweat lined her brow. Having lived in Phoenix, Arizona, for the past five years, she wasn't used to such chilly temperatures. She hadn't expected them here – at least not yet. It was August.

The house groaned with each gust of wind. Each

groan was followed by the sound of giant, calloused fingers scraping against a window. Just leaves on small branches, she told herself unconvincingly. The eerie hoot of an owl jarred her even more. Still, she continued to listen. All she wanted to hear was the crunching of dirt and gravel under the tires of their car. If there were a pizza in that car, even a cold one, so much the better.

AT FIRST LIGHT, Hannah opened her eyes. She surveyed the dreary, chilly room, half expecting to find Rick crashed on the sofa directly across from her. Surely he'd be there, probably tired, hopefully not hung-over, and ready to relate his adventure – or misadventure.

He wasn't there. Beyond the sound of breathing in and out, the only evidence of life was the twittering of a few songbirds outside in nearby trees. On most days, she'd be delighted by this cheerful sound, but not today. She listened for Rick's footsteps walking in the door, water raining down from the shower, something, anything.

Hannah struggled upright, her body stiff from spending the night huddled on the small loveseat. She stretched her arms and rolled her neck, attempting to clear her mind and lessen the discomfort. The combination of Rick's tardiness and a ranch house where nothing worked properly had taken her far beyond the boundaries of her limited comfort zone. What should she do? What *could* she do? No phone, no car. She couldn't clean even if she wanted to. She'd found no cleaning products, not even a disgusting old sponge under the sink. Didn't every household have one of those?

By 9:00 a.m., she could no longer ignore the queasy feeling in her empty stomach. She needed to expand her search for food, but she wasn't feeling up to venturing into the basement yet. According to every grisly horror movie, a dark, strange basement was a place to avoid.

Instead, she sat on the steps of the back porch that overlooked the beautiful valley, elbows on her knees, chin supported by the palms of her hands, and willed herself to relax. Only one good thought came to mind. *The house and all this land belong to me.*

That fact alone made her dizzy. The only thing she'd ever owned had been a run-down, old Ford Focus. On the bright side, at least it wasn't a Pinto. Now, she was a landowner and the mistress of a Colorado ranch. She should be thrilled, but no, she felt like a fish out of water – a very lonely fish.

THREE

Trace had almost given up. He'd received no reply to his knocks or his shouts, and he didn't have time to wait around. With his primary mission accomplished, he headed toward the truck.

"Come on, Oatie. Let's go."

The dog poked his fox-like face around the far corner of the house, barked, then turned and disappeared. Apparently, the red-speckled heeler had something more important to do than "go." But it was unlike Oatie to disobey such a simple command. Intrigued, Trace left the truck and went to see what the dog was up to.

Oatie stood on all fours, his tail drawing circles in the air, seemingly excited with what he'd found. That's when Trace saw her. He stared boldly, struck by her appearance. Striding closer and removing his cowboy hat, he said, "I see you've met my dog." He reached out to shake her hand but got no response. "My name's Trace. Trace McAllister."

Feeling awkward, he withdrew his unshaken hand. The young woman didn't say a word. She didn't even blink.

"You must be Hannah. Is Rick around?"

Either he was invisible, speaking a foreign language, or her ability to hear was limited. Could this pretty gal be on drugs? He hoped not. He repeated his words a little louder but still received no reaction. Dammit! His list of chores was long, and he needed to get going.

"Well, miss, I've brought the livestock according to the deal. The horses are in the front corral, and the cows—"

She glanced up and looked him right in eye. "Cows?"

"Yes, ma'am," he said slowly. "Two horses, four cows, and six hens. They're all in your charge as of today."

The young gal's startled expression made him grin. He felt certain she was not from around here. Probably just another city slicker acting out a fantasy, but this one seemed confused.

Oatie sat down beside her, and she rubbed his ears. *That's odd.* Trace frowned, scratching his head. The dog usually spent a little more time getting to know a stranger before he'd cozy up like that. But there he was, quite content with her hands on his ears. *Hmm. Lucky dog.*

He put his hat back on his head. "Here's my phone number," he said, handing her a well-worn card from his back pocket. "Have Rick give me a call. When do you expect him?"

Her answer was slow in coming, making him wonder if she'd overdosed on sleep aids, or had jet-lag, or something. He tried to make sense of her lack of communication. She was definitely out of it.

"I… I don't know," Hannah replied, her voice soft and fragile.

Oatie licked her cheek. She actually smiled, and her face lit up; it almost glowed. Trace couldn't help but notice her bright green eyes and her long blond ponytail. Then her sweet smile disappeared, the serious – or was it sad? – expression returned. Her pretty eyes looked up at him again, and words spilled from her lips.

"I have no phone, no electricity, no food, and no transportation."

With each word, the volume of her voice faded until it was nothing more than a whisper. Trace never had much talent when it came to comforting women, but he couldn't leave her like this.

Though her dilemma made no sense to him, he said,

"This is a small town, I'll make some calls and get the electricity and the landline turned on for you. Sorry, but it seems Rick misunderstood his responsibilities. Here, take my ranch phone for now."

She didn't reach for it, so he set it down beside her.

"Is someone delivering the animals' feed today?"

He knew the horses, Lewissa and Clark, would not be happy without their oats. In fact, they could make the young woman's life more miserable than it already was. Fortunately, the cows would be content eating grass in the lower pasture for now.

He raised his voice, needing an answer. "Hannah, I didn't see any feed for the animals. You're expecting it today, right?"

Her shining green eyes appeared dazed and on the brink of tears. He hoped she wouldn't cry. When a woman cried, it turned him inside out. A feeling he wanted no part of.

"I don't know. Rick took care of all those things."

She was an odd one for sure. Pretty, though. No, that wasn't quite right. She was beautiful, like a young Gwyneth Paltrow. Oatie's head now lay in Hannah's lap. He seemed content, even happy to remain there. Trace shifted his weight from one boot to the other, not sure what to do or say.

"I'll do what I can to help you with the animals until

your husband arrives," he offered, "but I've got to take the hens back. Without feed, those birds won't stick around. I can't stick around either. We're shorthanded again. Tell you what, since you've got my ranch phone, you can call my cell number if you need me. I'll be back tomorrow with some feed for all the animals."

He frowned, feeling helpless, and hoped her husband showed up soon. "Come on, Oatie," he said and headed back toward his truck.

What have I gotten myself into?

THE DOG GAVE Hannah another lick on her cheek before following Trace. She watched them walk away. Who was that cowboy, that good-looking cowboy? She shook her head and shoved her observation aside. This was not the time for frivolous thoughts about a handsome man. After all, her friend was still missing.

If this had happened in Phoenix, Hannah wouldn't have worried. There, Rick had a full-time job as a waiter, and he often played street basketball with several guy friends. He'd meet anyone, anytime, at any watering hole. Back home, it hadn't been unusual for several days to pass without seeing him, especially during the workweek.

But this was not Phoenix. This was a remote area of

Colorado inhabited by ranchers and the occasional hermit occupying a primitive cabin. At least that's what she'd heard. Now, with each passing moment, concern for Rick's safety gnawed at her gut and clouded her thinking.

I must do something. I can't just sit on these steps all day.

She stood up a little too quickly, and her world began to spin. Grabbing the rough-edged railing to keep from falling, it dawned on her that she'd had nothing more than wine and water since yesterday's lunchtime burger on the road – a logical excuse for the dizziness. She needed to eat. There had to be a can of something edible lying around.

There were still a few rooms and closets to explore, as well as the barns and stalls. She might even venture into the basement now that the midday sun beamed brightly above, and she had a phone – a *ranch* phone. How was that different from her cell phone? She picked up the strange, clunky object to make a 911 call. Easier said than done. It worked nothing like her cell phone. Frustrated, she vowed to try again a little later.

After an hour spent in dusty closets, cupboards, and drawers, she craved cleaning products almost as much as food. A knock at the front door put an end to that ridiculous thought. She hesitated. No one knew she was here except Trace and Rick. Rick wouldn't knock, and Trace had said he wouldn't be back until tomorrow. She peeked out the window closest to the door and spotted a middle-aged man.

"Pizza delivery," he called out.

He might as well have shouted *land shark*.

Hannah squinted at his face, trying to decide if the man looked trustworthy or not. He *was* carrying something that resembled a pizza box, but that made no sense. Home delivery way out here? No way. Did he think she was that gullible? She promptly reached over and locked the deadbolt.

FOUR

"Come on, lady," the man said, exasperation evident in his tone. "Open up. I have a pizza for someone named Hannah. Is that you?"

Could Rick have set this up? He was quite the jokester. Maybe she'd find a note inside the box. Her shoulders slumped. No. As much as she wished that were true, her head could not wrap around that scenario.

"No one delivers pizza this far from town." She spoke with enough confidence to make any man think twice about causing her harm. Who was she kidding?

"They do if Mr. McAllister places the order."

McAllister? Her thoughts rewound. *Trace McAllister.* Why would a ranch hand go to the trouble of sending her a pizza?

A gentle breeze carried the spicy aroma of honest-to-goodness pizza through the window, and hunger defeated caution. Hannah yanked the door open and took charge of the pizza box. Fumbling around in her pocket, she took out a couple of dollars and tried to tip the man, but he refused to accept her money.

By the time the man's vehicle was out of sight, she'd devoured her first slice and was reaching for a second. The pizza was out-of-this-world delicious. Before long, only half of it remained in the box. She hadn't even bothered to pick off the pepperoni.

That was the best pizza I've ever eaten, pepperoni and all, she thought, closing the box. With the feeding frenzy over, she felt physically stronger and ready to give that darn phone another try.

Hoping to renew her spirit, she sat on the front porch breathing in the fresh, cool mountain air with the phone in hand. She explored its numerous buttons but suddenly stopped, distracted by her uncanny ability to notice the subtlest of scents. Horses?

Glancing to her left, she spotted the two horses Trace had delivered earlier standing in the corral not far from the house. They seemed perfectly at ease, swishing their tails at flies and lowering their mouths to the soft green grass.

As far as she could recall, she'd never been in the presence or scent range of a real live horse before, and she hadn't expected their smell to be so pleasant. Now that she lived in the high country of Colorado, she suspected that many new scents would tickle her nose and, possibly, bring her joy. Hannah watched the horses until the sun dipped below the mountaintop and the evening chill returned.

Back inside, Rick's absence dominated her thinking once again. If only he'd return, she could get on with reinventing her life, and he could begin his cowboy experience. She longed to set up an art studio – just the sound of that made her smile – and resume drawing, only this time with true dedication. After that, she might dive into a new project: concocting essential oils. That would require some research as well as the planting of an herb garden.

Hannah picked up the clunky cell phone again, *ranch phone*, she corrected herself, when a new thought struck her, making her pause. *What if Rick ditched me or changed his mind about our hastily made plans?* She blinked, stunned at the possibility. No. He'd been just as excited as her about the opportunity to transform his dream into reality. He wouldn't bail out on that, would he?

Maybe, he was suddenly uncomfortable with the thought that she'd put up all the money for their adventure. She closed her eyes and took a deep breath, pushing those distressing ideas from her mind but also realizing that the alternatives were likely far worse. She needed to think, take some action, but instead, surrendering to mental exhaustion, she slipped into a deep, dark sleep.

AS THE EARLY morning sun streamed through the window, Hannah stretched, uncurling from her spot on the loveseat. Another night had passed without incident or Rick's return, but because she'd met two of the locals – Trace and the pizza guy – she faced this new day feeling slightly more hopeful than anxious.

With curiosity, she flipped one of the light switches, then squealed with joy when the overhead light went on. Electricity! In the corner of the room sat an ancient-looking telephone, and she dared herself to pick it up. *Voila!* A dial tone.

"Yes!" she said, high-fiving the air. "The little things in life really do make a difference."

Her giddiness was short-lived, however, overtaken by her ongoing concern for Rick's welfare. But now that she had a regular phone, she could call the authorities and get him some help if that's what he needed.

The sound of energetic barking interrupted her call. Half undressed and determined not to embarrass herself, she quickly wrapped the one and only blanket around her like a beach towel and made it to the door just in time to greet her visitors. The ranch hand and his adorable dog stood side-by-side, one smiling, the other wagging its tail.

"Good mornin', sunshine. Sleep well?"

Today, Hannah took a good look at the cowboy's face. "As well as can be expected. Good morning to you too," she said politely, matching his smile. "Thank you for the pizza."

"You're welcome," he replied, tipping his hat and widening his grin. He looked slightly puzzled, though. Probably due to her change in demeanor. She'd acted like a zombie when they'd first met. "I was hoping you and Rick would join me for a lesson on how to store the feed and how to dispense it to the animals."

Holding the blanket tightly around her, she sighed. "He hasn't made it back yet, though I expect him any minute."

Trace frowned and took a step back. "Okay." His eyes followed the blanket dress she wore. "I can see you're not quite ready for that kind of activity anyway. So I'll take care of —"

"Give me ninety seconds, and I will be."

She closed the door, grabbed yesterday's clothes, and ran to the bathroom. With her bare hand, she wiped the grime off the mirror, then stared at her reflection. There stood a woman in desperate need of a shower, clean hair, and lip-gloss. Oh, well. After dressing quicker than a runway model, she added a baseball cap and sunglasses, then dashed out the door for ranch lesson number one.

Enjoying the view of the handsome and obviously strong cowboy, Hannah stood back and watched Trace unload and store the feed. The chickens scurried in and around the open horse stalls, pecking and scratching at every little crumb. *They really do say bok-bok!* Until today, she'd thought only cartoon chickens made that sound.

"This should last about a week," Trace told her. "Now, let's feed these critters."

He took her through the necessary steps, then frowned at the hens. "Are you sure you want just six? I'd be more comfortable if you had one more."

Hannah gave him a sideways squint, unsure.

"I could bring you a rooster. Then you'd have eggs *and* chicks. You could sell them. People do buy them, you know."

"I did not come to Colorado to run a chicken ranch," she said matter-of-factly with her hands on her hips.

Their eyes met, and Hannah blushed. "Sorry. That didn't come out quite right."

He didn't laugh out loud, but she detected a subtle grin pushing at the corners of his mouth. Avoiding her eyes, he turned back to the business of opening the bag of oats, and she let herself admire the strong, lean line of his body, his snug jeans, his—*What is wrong with me?*

Their conversation came to an abrupt halt at the sound of an approaching vehicle. Seconds later, an unfamiliar SUV turned in and parked.

"It's the sheriff."

"Good! I can tell him about Rick's absence. Maybe he knows something."

Trace looked down at her, his eyes dark with concern. "Well, he's a *she*." He scratched his head. "And a house call from her is never good."

A petite, auburn-haired woman stepped out of the car and headed toward them. Her face showed no expression, but as she drew closer, she studied Hannah and the surroundings.

"Hey there, Jane. Don't often see you out this far from town."

"There's been an accident."

Hannah, at a loss for words, gasped. Her body shivered with an uncomfortable chill assuming the sheriff's news would go from bad to worse. *This is about Rick.*

Trace stepped in. "What kind of accident?" he said, glancing sideways at Hannah.

Jane folded her arms and pursed her lips in thought, her eyes shifting from Trace to Hannah and back.

"Come on, Jane, tell us what you know," urged Trace.

"Actually," she said with a huff, and looking directly at Hannah, "I'm here to find out what *you* know." Just like her expression, the woman's words lacked emotion.

Finding her voice, Hannah's response trailed out. "I… I don't know much. Rick and I drove here two days ago. We came inside and toasted our new home with a few sips of wine. He drove back into town to pick up a pizza and… and he still hasn't returned. That's all I know."

As the seriousness of the situation hit Hannah, her breathing sped up. Stars blinked in her darkening vision, and she caught herself stumbling sideways. During her teenage years, she developed a predisposition to feel light-headed when her stress level soared, but she hoped the cool Colorado air would help with that inconvenient affliction.

"Is he hurt or in jail? I want to see him." Her voice trembled at the thought of her good friend in trouble before he'd had a chance to explore their new home.

Jane looked at Trace, then at Hannah, then back to Trace. "I'm afraid you can't do that," she said, unfolding her arms and shoving her hands into her pockets. "It seems the car veered off the road, rolled down a steep embankment, then crashed and burned." The sheriff paused and took a deep breath. "At this point, we assume the charred body we found is that of your husband."

Hearing the talk of a charred body sent Hannah reeling, and she slumped to the ground. Disoriented, she felt as if she were floating, floating upward. As near consciousness returned, she saw blurred light and shadows and heard the sound of muffled voices. She also felt cradled by strong, warm arms. Trace.

"I'll check back later," Jane told him, then headed out.

He gazed down, his steel-blue eyes displaying concern. "You okay?"

"I… I think so," Hannah mumbled. "I feel so fuzzy, lightheaded. Did I pass out?"

Trace kept quiet, but Oatie whimpered and put his chin on her thigh.

"This sometimes happens when I get stressed and breath too fast, " she continued, her voice trailing off as she remembered the sheriff's words, and sat up straight.

Rick was dead.

Reality hit her hard. Her lips trembled as tears streamed down her face.

"I'm sorry, Hannah," Trace said, running a soothing hand over her back. "I can't even imagine what it would be like to lose a husband … or any loved one, so suddenly."

Hannah shook her head. "No. It's not like that," she said in between breaths, trying to regain control. "Rick isn't, I mean, wasn't my husband or even my boyfriend. There were days when I didn't like him. He would drive me crazy, you know?" she rambled. "But he was my best friend, and we had a plan. Our dreams were finally coming true," she said, her eyes swelling with tears again as she looked up at Trace. "We had a deal. Why would he go and ruin everything?"

Trace looked back, his eyes warm and understanding. "Jane said it was an accident. I doubt it was his idea to be in a deadly car crash."

"Your right. That was a selfish comment I made."

With a subtle nod, he urged her to go on.

"It's complicated," continued Hannah with a gulp. "You see, I won some money in the lottery."

Trace's eyebrows rose, but he didn't speak.

"My bad-luck life had finally turned around. I never had money before, and as weird as this sounds, I was totally stressed out, not knowing how to handle it or what to do with it. So, when Rick came up with a plan where we'd each get a do-over to create better lives, I jumped on it. All that stress melted away – until just now. "

She stared straight ahead, trying to believe the unbelievable. She imagined Rick's laughing eyes and his familiar teasing smile, and her eyes clouded with tears again. There was a sudden hole, a deep void in her chest, leaving her feeling oddly displaced and sorry for her friend's untimely death. Several moments passed before she could speak again.

"So here I am, a city girl who went dancing every weekend, in the middle of nowhere. And now he's gone, forever. I'm alone with two horses, four cows, and a whole bunch of chickens." She sighed, reaching down to pat Oatie's head. "What am I supposed to do? My dream was simple: I just wanted time to draw, to plant a garden, and to live somewhere nicer than my small Phoenix apartment." Looking at the room, she sniffed and then added, "I think it will take me a year just to clean up this place."

She looked up at Trace, the stranger providing silent comfort. His eyes were gentle, his expression soft with sympathy.

"Thanks for staying with me." She placed her cool, slender hand on top of his warm, rough one. Neither hand moved.

"Not a problem. I do have several appointments in town, but I can cancel them if you—"

She shook her head. "I need some time to think. Thanks for your offer, though."

He stood, ending their brief physical contact. Oatie bounced to his side, and the pair walked quietly out the front door. Except that he was handsome and kind, Hannah knew next to nothing about this cowboy. Still, she could not imagine coping with the current situation without him. She sat for a moment taking in the rugged scent that lingered on the palm of her hand – a trace of Trace.

A horse whinnied, interrupting her tenuous state of mind, and she rose to her feet. *I might as well get to know my animals.* She stepped out onto the front porch and cast her eyes over the vastness of the ranch – *it's my land,* she reminded herself. But this was not the life she'd wished for. This was Rick's wish, Rick's dream. With nothing better to do, she'd tagged along. Now, she was alone… except for the animals.

Taking a deep breath, Hannah walked closer to the corral. The mare – *Lewissa*, Trace had called her – meandered over, seeming curious.

"Hello," she said softly, reaching up to pat the horse's nose. "I'm Hannah, and I'm here to deliver the news that you're stuck with me."

The horse's ears twitched as she spoke, taking in the sound of her voice.

"I hope you'll forgive my rookie mistakes. You see, I've become both a novice rancher and a fake widow today." She tilted her head, loosening the tense muscles in her neck. "How many people can say that, huh?"

The mare blinked, then stomped the ground once with her front hoof. Hannah eyed the horse with humorous suspicion. "That's right, Lewissa. You know only one."

FIVE

Trace sipped hot, black coffee at the local diner, lost in restless thoughts of the past two days. He hadn't noticed Callie until she'd slid into his booth and sat directly across from him. Every other guy in the diner likely noticed her presence from the get-go. The teenager oozing sexuality looked him up and down while twirling a long lock of wild red hair between two brightly painted fingernails.

"Hey, Trace," she said, smacking a wad of gum. "You're looking serious this morning. What's up?"

"Callie." He nodded. "Got plans today?"

She wrinkled her nose and raised one speculative eyebrow. "Nothin' I can't change." She flashed him the flirty smile she'd been working on since the age of twelve. "What do you have in mind? A picnic? A romantic ride to your upper pasture?" Then biting her lip and batting her long lashes, added, "Or maybe your lower pasture?"

He leaned back in the booth to increase the distance between them. "Nope. We need a little help at the ranch. That new hired hand didn't work out." He shrugged. "He wasn't much good anyway, but now we're shorthanded. I need you to feed and water the animals near the main barns and over at the east pasture for a few weeks. The stalls could use a little mucking too."

Her exaggerated look of contemplation surprised him, as did her hesitation. She'd always agreed to his requests. Had she added the art of negotiation to her instinctive talent for manipulation?

"Well—" she said slowly, stretching out the word, putting her rarely used Texas accent into the mix.

"You can stay in the small bunkhouse. It's currently unoccupied."

She blew him a kiss, apparently satisfied. "I'll head right over."

"Uh, Callie? Put on some appropriate clothing first, okay? And there's one more thing." He reached into his pocket for his wallet. "Pick up some groceries and cleaning products and take them to the woman now living at the Lucky 7."

Trace handed the teen a fist full of cash just as Sheriff

Jane Carter walked through the door. Seeing her, Callie scooted out and waved a quick good-bye as the sheriff took her place in the booth.

"You know she's trouble, right?"

"Of course. No worries. I'm immune to her kind of trouble. After my last relationship, I'm not looking for another. Especially not with a young filly like her."

"Maybe not, but I know for a fact that she has you in her sights. Always has. She's not about to give up, either."

"And just how do you know that?"

Her expression was one of reluctant resignation. "Well, in addition to observing my daughter's behavior all her life, let's just say that her plans for you are the main plot in her diary."

Trace raised one eyebrow. "You read her diary?" he said, his mouth twisting into a wry smile. "Been snooping around, huh?"

Unapologetic, Jane said, "That's my nature. Besides, sometimes she leaves it sitting on her bed, wide open. Hey, I'd be a fool not to take a look." She frowned. "Callie did mention someone named Buddy recently. So maybe you've got competition, cowboy."

"Bet I know why you're here," Trace said, changing the subject. "Got more news about the accident?"

She didn't answer his question but asked, "Did you

talk with the wife?"

"There is no wife."

"What?"

"They weren't married, just friends, platonic friends sharing the property. She mentioned something about winning a lottery and looking for a new place to live. I got the impression that her friend wanted to play cowboy, and she wanted nothing more than to draw pictures and get out of the Phoenix heat."

The sheriff scowled. "Huh. Then I've got a problem. I need to notify next of kin and find out where to send the remains. Do you know Rick's last name? And don't tell me it's Smith."

"Okay. I won't." He took his time answering her question. "I'm pretty sure Rick's surname was Johnson."

"Johnson? Come on. No kidding?" She shook her head, disgusted. "That's no better than Smith when it comes to narrowing down my search. Oh, hell." Her deep sigh sounded tired. "I need to talk with Hannah. Got a few more questions for her. Then I hope to tie up a few loose ends and get this case wrapped up."

Jane continued to bend Trace's ear, thinking out loud about the accident, for another twenty minutes. The two had known each other for a long time, and they talked openly. That's how it was.

"One thing bothers me," she said. "I saw no evidence

of the car braking, swerving, or taking any action to avoid going off the road and over the cliff." She shook her head. "I know they'd driven a long way, and I suppose he could have fallen asleep, but – I don't know. Something's just not right."

"Trust your gut, Jane. That's what you're always telling me to do. Got plans for an autopsy?"

"I doubt I could get approval for that. There's no real evidence of foul play and no family member demanding one." She regarded him curiously. "Say, you interested in checking out the crash site? Maybe you'll see something I missed. You're pretty good with details."

Trace had to admit he was intrigued, but he had one more place to be before returning to check on Hannah. He agreed to follow Jane to the scene of the accident, knowing he would return later for an in-depth inspection.

Ten miles outside of town, she pulled over, and Trace parked his truck behind her patrol car. A broken aspen sapling, looking rather forlorn, stood at the site, providing a landmark of sorts. Not trusting his ability to find this same small, damaged tree later, he tied a piece of rope to one of the low branches on a large blue spruce just a few yards away.

"Thanks," Jane said as she waved and pulled away.

Trace climbed into his truck. "No problem," he mumbled to himself.

HANNAH JUMPED AT THE SUDDEN, slamming sound, then scolded herself for being so on edge. Convinced the wind must have blown one of the doors open, she hurried first to check the front door, then stopped short. A curvy teenager in tight, skinny jeans and a flimsy, purple tank top a few sizes too small stood in her kitchen, loaded down with plastic bags.

Hannah eyed her warily. "Can I help you? I think you might be in the wrong house."

"Nope. I'm right where I should be. Not so sure about you, though."

From the moment their eyes connected, animosity filled the air. Hannah had no idea why, but she did know the teenager hadn't even knocked. She'd barged right in as if she owned the place.

"What do you want?" Hannah asked, backing away. Something about the girl's appearance and demeanor made her uncomfortable.

Setting the bags on the kitchen island, this uninvited stranger pulled her shirt down to cover her navel and tugged her pants up slightly above her hips. Even so, there was far too much skin showing in Hannah's opinion. Even when she'd gone to the dimly lit dance clubs, she never flashed that much flesh.

"My name's Callie," the girl snapped, putting one hand on her hip, tapping her boot-covered foot with impatience. "What do I want? To get back to Trace. We're a team, and he needs me. But the real question is: What do *you* need?" She regarded Hannah with a cruel, critical eye. "Looks like you need a little bit of everything, starting with a shower and a total makeover. Have you looked in a mirror lately?"

Hannah glared at the girl, stunned by her rudeness. How dare she walk into Hannah's ranch house and insult her like that? Maybe, on another day, Hannah would've taken her on, sniped right back at her with something clever and equally cutting, but today was not that day. She had neither the physical nor the mental strength.

"Are ya just gonna stand there?" The girl swept her hands impatiently toward the driveway. "I've got more bags in the truck, and they're all for you. Get a move-on. I don't have all day. Like I said, Trace is waitin' for me."

They unloaded the remainder of the bags, and to Hannah's delight, they contained groceries and cleaning products. *Trace*. This had to have been his idea. First the pizza, now this. Though grateful for his thoughtfulness, she couldn't help wishing he'd sent a less toxic delivery person or, better yet, brought the supplies himself.

"How long ya gonna stick around?

"I don't know. A month, a year." Hannah suddenly

found a bit of strength, and she shrugged. "Maybe forever."

"You won't like it here," Callie warned, using an unmistakable, mean-girl tone and a wagging finger. "There's nothing to do, not many people around, and the winters – oh, man, you're gonna hate the winters. Your power will go out, you'll get snowed in, and your pipes will freeze." Her eyes widened with excitement. "Do ya know what that means? Do ya?"

Hannah didn't know and, right now, she didn't care.

"Well," she continued, condescension dripping from her lips, "the water will freeze. And when the water freezes, you can't flush." The girl actually grinned at her. "Nope. You're not gonna make it through the first winter. I'd bet money on that. A ranch is no place for someone like you."

This teen is about to bring out the worst in me. I can feel it, Hannah thought and bit her lower lip to keep from lashing back. For someone who'd been in such a hurry to get going, the obnoxious girl lingered. She chattered away, going on about the weather and other things that didn't matter. Hannah prayed this was not an example of a typical Stillwater local.

Hannah scrutinized her visitor and thought she recognized something familiar in her mannerisms. Had she come face-to-face with the country version of her former, party-girl self? Not that she'd ever been a rude person, but she certainly hadn't been a good friend or given the time of day to anyone but Rick.

She'd been so caught up surviving in her own little world, she'd rarely given much thought to the needs of others. Her previous goals were pitiful: To pay her rent and to have people tell her she was "cool" at the dance clubs. Hannah did not like the selfish image that formed in her mind, and she vowed to create a more purposeful life for herself. She just needed a little more time.

Her thoughts wandered, and now she had a few questions of her own. What was the teen's connection to Trace? Was she a relative? A little sister? A neighbor? A girlfriend? She cringed inwardly and refused to let herself imagine Trace with this... this sexy little brat.

After the teen finally walked out the door, Hannah set to work emptying the shopping bags' contents onto the counter. Paper towels, a large container of all-purpose liquid cleaner, a dustpan with a brush, a can of furniture polish, and a bag of rags. The sorely needed cleaning process could soon begin. But one of the teen's questions nagged at her. How long would she stay here? Perhaps there would be no need to transform this place from a dusty, ill-kept house into her very own clean and tidy, furnished home.

She'd file that question for the time being and explore

the contents of the grocery bags. They'd been heavy. When she peered inside, she discovered why. The bags contained mostly cans: cans of vegetables, soup, fruit, tuna, and meat. Canned meat? Her stomach twisted at the thought. She didn't eat fresh meat products and didn't think she could eat canned meat even if she were starving. Fortunately, the teen had brought a six-pack of soda, a loaf of white bread, two bags of chips, a jar of instant coffee, and – thank goodness – a bag of apples. Real apples.

If nothing else, Callie had been a distraction. While the girl prattled on, Rick's deadly accident had slipped briefly from Hannah's thoughts. Now, alone once again, reality rushed back in.

As a child, Hannah and her mom had moved so often that she'd never established any lasting friendships. She'd had dozens of casual acquaintances back in Phoenix where she'd been the weekend party girl, but other than Rick, she had no one she could call a friend.

Hannah needed another distraction. Right on cue, the horses whinnied as if calling her to come out and play. Cleaning and organizing could wait.

The top rail of the corral's fence made a perfect perch, so she climbed up and watched the animals from that vantage point. Lewissa was magnificent: golden in color with a thick, creamy mane. Her partner, Clark, was a dark copper color and just as beautiful. They stood side-by-side, their heads close, their tails waving lazily. They were friends who appeared to be having a quiet conversation.

Rick never got to see his horses. He would have loved them. As Hannah wiped away a single tear, Lewissa turned and stepped toward her.

"Hello there, Lewissa. How's your day going?"

The mare puffed through her nose, sounding content, then came closer and nudged the skin on Hannah's arm with her soft, velvety lips. She stroked the horse's nose, surprised at how smooth it felt and how gentle the huge animal appeared to be. Then she rubbed the coarse hair between the mare's moist, brown eyes. Clark noticed the attention the mare now enjoyed, and he ambled over. She gave both horses pats and rubs. Just being near Lewissa and Clark lifted her spirits.

The serene moment vanished as the horses suddenly tensed, lifting their flared nostrils into the air. Clark muttered uneasily, then the two trotted briskly away to stand by the side of the stalls. Hannah glanced around, trying to figure out what had spooked them. She scanned the space between the house and the corral but saw nothing unusual. Had she done something wrong?

She waited, watching the horses for a few more minutes, then headed back inside. *I will download a book or two about horse behavior by the end of the day.* First, she'd clean the shelves and arrange the recently arrived food items. Then she'd find locations for her art supplies and her small collection of romance and post-apocalyptic paperback books, her favorite genres. The two framed photos she'd brought with her deserved an extra special spot. One was a picture of Rick and her, posing on the dance floor of their favorite nightclub. The other, a treasured photo of her mother standing beside Hannah at her high school graduation five years ago.

Staring at the photo brought back memories of that significant, bittersweet day. Her mom had asked, "Hannah, are you happy?" Before she came up with an answer, her mom added, "You deserve better, more than I have given you."

Hannah loved her mom, but the words she spoke that night felt unsettling. What was she getting at?

"It would bring me joy, even peace of mind if you chose to explore the world as well as yourself. In fact, I insist that you do."

Thoughts of creating a life on her own began with that first nudge from her mom.

And now, today, here she was, wiping her arm across her forehead, clearing away the grimy sweat. Enough for now. Break time. Just as she opened the fridge to grab a soda, the phone rang, causing her to jump. She'd forgotten about the working landline. But who could it be? No one knew her number yet. Heck, she didn't even know it.

"Hello?"

"Hi, Hannah, it's Trace."

"Hi. It seems you know my phone number even before me. Mind sharing?"

He laughed, relayed the number, then asked, "Mind if I stop by?"

How could she say no to such a handsome, helpful man? "Of course not. Come on over. I'll be here, guaranteed."

Where else would she be? Stillwater was the only town around, and she didn't have a car. She didn't even have a bicycle.

"Did you get the groceries?"

"Oh, I got them all right. Groceries and a whole lot more."

Trace hesitated. "Do I want to know what you mean by that?"

"Probably not, but I'm going to tell you anyway. The delivery girl talked mostly about herself but also asked about my plans. She seemed determined to know just how long I'd be staying at the ranch. After that, she proceeded to say everything she could think of to get me to leave. Weird, huh?"

He didn't reply. Had he not heard her? It hadn't been a rhetorical question.

"Trace?"

"Yeah?"

"Sometimes you don't have much to say, do you?"

He paused, maybe thinking about his words or hers. "Well, I find silence is seldom misquoted."

Now Hannah was the one with little to say. Neither would be misquoted for a while. Trace seemed comfortable with the lack of dialogue; Hannah, not so much.

"She spoke to me as if I was some kind of city-slicker idiot, you know? Even an enemy. She doesn't know me, but for some reason, she wants me gone."

Hannah heard him exhale and wondered if she or Callie had caused his obvious exasperation. "Sorry if she was unpleasant. The kid can be a headstrong handful, I should know."

The image of the belligerent redhead popped back into her mind, and she remembered the teen's stinging words. Trace's description of her was an understatement, to say the least.

"A headstrong handful, huh? Okay. See you soon."

Rude, unpredictable, hazardous to my health. That's how I'd describe her.

SIX

Trace pulled up beside Hannah's ranch, house though not yet ready to face her. She'd seemed angry, and he didn't want to deal with that. Oatie got up in his face and barked. "All right. Here we go." He stepped from the truck's cab and then held the door open, so Oatie could jump out. He didn't have to wait long; the dog couldn't get out fast enough.

As soon as he saw Hannah waiting for them on the porch, Oatie sprinted over, wagging his tail in obvious joy. Hannah's whole face lightened when she greeted him, softening into the prettiest smile Trace had ever seen. Those two behaved as if they'd been together forever.

Studying his dog, Trace wished he'd paid more attention to him earlier. Oatie was a good judge of character, and he'd taken to Hannah from the first moment they'd met. The dog had always been uneasy around that incompetent ranch hand. The guy had been worthless, and Oatie had known that right away too.

Hannah led Oatie toward a bench near the corral. The dog trotted at her side like an overgrown puppy instead of the brilliant, macho cattle dog that he was. She looked different today. Her long blond hair hung loose, catching the late afternoon sun, and the air around her glowed like a halo. She looked good, too good, wearing a sleeveless white blouse and faded jeans. He'd never seen a woman look so sexy and angelic at the same time.

She glanced toward him in invitation, raising her slender arms to show him she had a bottle of soda in each hand. He blinked disconcerted. He hadn't realized he'd been staring.

Good grief! Now, who's the puppy dog? And a panting one, at that. Shake it off, man!

Trace ran his fingers through his chestnut-colored hair, then ambled over to the bench where Oatie, Hannah, and a cold soda awaited.

"What's up?" she asked, handing him the bottle. She patted the spot next to her on the bench. Still feeling somewhat like a dog, he obeyed and sat.

"Just wanted to make sure you were okay, and it

seems that you are. Oh, and the sheriff was wondering if you knew how to reach Rick's family."

Hannah's lips tightened, and her beautiful smile faded. He wished he hadn't brought up the topic of Rick so quickly, but there it was. She said nothing and merely shook her head.

"Your best friend never mentioned any family?"

"No," she said, her green eyes bright and inviting just moments before now hardened into a glare. "What's this all about?"

"They need to notify next of kin, that's all."

She looked away, embarrassed. "Sorry. No, Rick never mentioned anyone." After a moment, she cleared her throat. "I want to hold a memorial service for him. It's the least I can do."

Trace kept his opinion to himself as long as possible, but when Hannah didn't elaborate, he spoke up.

"I think you should give it a little more time."

The glare was back, but he continued anyway. "I know he was your friend, but think about it. You don't know his friends or how to contact them. You don't even know if he has family or where they might live. No one would attend the service."

"You and I would attend. And Rick would be there in spirit. It's not about the number of attendees, you know. And I could begin searching for friends and family. They might exist." Her head nodded with assurance. "A memorial service is the right thing to do."

Maybe she was right, so he dropped the subject, for now.

"I'm headed over to the scene of the accident to take a look around while there's still some daylight. The car and the – uh," He cleared his throat and tried again. "Everything has been removed, so I'll likely just see some scorched earth. Jane suggested I take a look. You're welcome to ride along."

Trace regretted his invitation immediately. Her feelings about the accident, the death, and her life without Rick were still understandably raw. What would she think of his insensitive proposal?

"Sure. I'll go with you," she said to his surprise, then continued hesitantly, "But I hate to leave the animals alone."

"Don't worry; they'll be fine. They like to be left alone now and then."

A slight crease appeared between Hannah's fair eyebrows. "I meant to tell you that Lewissa seemed upset today. I couldn't figure out why, though."

"Huh. That's not like her. And I've known Lewissa since birth," Trace said. "If it makes you feel better, I'll check her out before we go," he added, already heading towards where the mare was standing.

With a quick one-two and a measured jump, Trace mounted the horse within seconds, requiring no saddle, no bit, or reins, and rode her out of the corral at a slow trot. He led her around the ranch house a few times, giving her free rein so that he could feel her mood, applying subtle pressure with his legs to guide her when necessary.

Lewissa, in return, obeyed but appeared reluctant each time they turned toward the back of the house, craning her neck around to look toward Hannah. Trace was puzzled but decided, as he often did, to keep his thoughts to himself. He told Hannah he found nothing unusual with Lewissa's behavior, other than the horse seemed to like her as much as the dog did.

"Good," said Hannah with a sigh of relief as Trace jumped down and led the mare back to the corral. "Okay then, let's go."

They arrived at the site in less than thirty minutes. As soon as they stepped from the truck, Hannah froze in her tracks and put her hand over her mouth, her eyes wide. Slowly, she lowered her hand and let her eyes roam the area. "There's death here, I can feel it," she said in a hushed voice. Then, as if smelling food from the oven, she sniffed the air and confirmed in a firm tone, "I smell death."

Her reaction and unexpected comment stopped Trace

in his tracks. "Well, someone died down there," he said, pointed over the steep hill.

"Yes, but I smell death up here on the road. Doesn't that seem odd?"

He regarded her skeptically. "Now I've seen everything, a woman who can out-sniff Oatie." He chuckled, then got serious. "That's not possible. Death would have occurred sometime *after* the impact of the crash."

Oatie sniffed the air, his snout moving up and down. He also smelled something. Although not as quickly as Hannah, his agitation increased as he began to pace and leap around. Trace looked from Oatie to Hannah and back, shrugged, and started toward the spot that captured his dog's attention. He was a damn good tracker and fully trusted his dog's ability, maybe Hannah's too. As he got closer and walked a few steps past Oatie, Trace kept his eyes on the ground, following a short trail of black spots in the middle of the road. Oatie barked – one short, staccato-like woof – and then rushed past him, his nose to the ground like a bloodhound. He stopped when he reached the darkest spots, tail wagging, drawing rapid circles in the air.

"What the hell?" cursed Trace as he stopped beside Oatie.

He stared at the spots, uncertain. They *could* be dried blood. Trace had no way of checking; he wasn't a detective and didn't possess their tricks of the trade. Oatie, on the other hand, had his own tricks, whether he knew it or not. Lifting his leg, he peed on several of the dark spots, transforming them into one small, reddish-brown puddle. Definitely blood. Rick's blood? That seemed like the logical conclusion.

As soon as Hannah joined him, her hand flew to her mouth, stifling the small groan that slipped from her throat. Trace shoved his hands into his pockets, resisting the uncharacteristic urge to put his arms around her. This recent discovery was disturbing. Until this moment, there had been no concrete reason or evidence to suggest any injury had occurred prior to the car veering off the road. If Trace had anticipated such a find, he never would have brought Hannah along.

"Come on. We should go," he said.

She stood stiffly, lifeless as a statue. "No."

Concerned at her trance-like state, he took her arm, but she pulled away and shook her head. "We must figure out what really happened."

He thought about reminding her that they weren't detectives, but from the expression on her face, he could see that wasn't going to make a difference.

"Okay," he said. "Wait here. I'll check out the site where the car ended up."

"I'm going with you," she said firmly, her tone coated with determination.

Despite his misgivings, Trace took her hand and helped her down the steep slope. When they arrived at the bottom of the ravine, he placed his hands on her shoulders, knowing this experience could be traumatic for her.

They stood in silence, staring at the charred bushes, small trees, and large rocks surrounding them. Even the ground was coated in black. Hannah leaned back, some of her weight relaxing against his body, and he automatically encircled her with his arms, enjoying her delicate, floral scent. She didn't move away.

ON THE RIDE back to her place, few words were spoken. Hannah felt the need to talk about Rick, the accident, and what might become of her, but she'd already figured out that Trace wasn't the chatty type. The only one who'd want to hear, and would listen patiently, was her mother. She'd know exactly what to say and what to do. But she wasn't here. Trace was her only friend now. Or was he just a thoughtful and extremely handsome neighbor?

Having nothing to lose, she asked, "Any thoughts? About the accident, I mean?"

Trace glanced at her with a look of contemplation. "Well, I try to never miss a good chance to keep quiet. It's safer that way." He paused, and his irresistible grin emerged.

She blinked at him, her usual quick wit nowhere to be found. "I see."

All eyes went back to the gravel road. A few minutes later, he drove right past her long dirt driveway.

"Hey, you missed the turn!"

"I know. My mechanical horse is headed toward the barn."

Hannah grinned. *What is it with this guy? This hunk of a cowboy. He isn't much of a talker, and when he does speak, he says the oddest things.*

"I'd like to go home," she declared, uncertain of his plans.

Trace chuckled. "Glad to hear you referring to the ranch as home."

"Go back," she insisted.

He applied the brakes and brought the truck to a complete stop right in the middle of the road. "I thought you might like to come for dinner at my place," he explained, turning to look at her, his smile more than a little charming. "Dinner will be ready by the time we get there, and I promise it'll be worth your time."

Hannah raised an eyebrow. "Hmm. So you put something in the Crockpot before you left this morning, huh?"

"That's one way to explain it."

She sighed, giving in. "I have no other dinner plans, but I warn you—" she started, but let her voice drop. *Who am I kidding? He probably knows I find him attractive, just like every other woman around here.*

They drove north along a gravel road that curved through areas of dense pine, open pastures, and aspen-covered hills. Every direction offered breath-taking beauty.

"Look there," he said, gesturing with his chin and cutting the truck's speed to a snail's pace.

Hannah gasped, thrilled by the sight of a doe, paused at the edge of the road, flanked by her two spotted fawns. By the time they reached the large ranch gate, she'd seen a total of nine deer, two marmots, a pair of red-tail hawks, a lone elk, and more chipmunks than she could count.

"Amazing. Is it always like this?"

"This time of year, this time of day, yeah. I'm just sorry you didn't get to see the bear."

"The bear? Oh, my. You're not worried about having bears as neighbors?"

He shook his head. "No. We just give a momma with cubs a wide berth. I worry far more about humans than I do about wildlife. But other humans rarely come up this far. If they did, they'd be trespassing, and I'd convince them to be on their way."

Hannah frowned, unsure of his intended meaning. She pushed her questions aside for now and used the time to enjoy the incredible sights before the sun dipped below the horizon. Dozens of brown, white-faced cows and their calves grazed in the distance, and a colorful herd of horses raised their heads, curious.

"What beautiful ranch land," she said in awe. "No matter which direction I look, it's like a sweeping scene from a western movie. You work here, right?"

He chuckled. "Yep. I do a lot of work here. Lord knows I've got the calluses to prove it." As if to prove it, he reached over and tickled her neck with his rough fingers.

She laughed softly and pulled away, then stared in disbelief at the biggest log home she'd ever seen. Or was it a hotel? He parked in front of the massive structure, and she gazed at him, confused, as he walked around to her side of the truck and opened the door.

"We're stopping here? Why?"

"Because you accepted my dinner invitation." He'd brought her to a dude ranch restaurant – that made sense. Or perhaps Trace had permission to bring her to his employer's ranch for this evening's meal. That made more sense and put her mind at ease. He took her by the hand, led her to the mammoth wooden door, and opened it – without knocking.

What is it with the people around here? Doesn't anyone knock?

The entryway was huge; *everything* was huge. Hannah stood in the doorway, speechless and small. She felt as if she were flipping through the pages of the slickest ranch magazine ever published, and she'd seen a few when Rick had been ranch shopping.

He dropped her hand and held out his arms. "Welcome to my ranch, my home. It's been in my family for generations. Come on. I'll show you around."

She blinked. "This is *your* ranch? All this time, I thought you were the local livestock delivery guy."

"I suppose I deserve that title. I did deliver your livestock. Under normal circumstances, I would have sent one of my ranch hands, but that guy flew the coup. He was a worthless hand anyway. Callie had more skill at fifteen than he did, and she was also dedicated to the cows. When her mom dropped her off to learn about ranching and helping out during round-ups, I'd have to insist she go home at the end of the day."

I seriously doubt her dedication was to the cows, thought Hannah as a crooked, un-amused smirk formed on her face.

"Rosa!" he called. "We've got a guest tonight."

Rosa? Hannah glanced around. *Was that his wife? Girlfriend? Mother?*

A woman walked into the dining room with an extra place setting and a welcoming smile. With relief, Hannah decided she looked a bit too old to be his love interest.

"Maybe that unskilled hand left because he didn't like my cooking," Rosa suggested, attempting to disguise her grin, then looked at Hannah. "Tonight is pasta and salad night. Hope you don't mind."

"Mind? That sounds delicious! My kind of meal."

Their dinner conversation revolved around Hannah's long, involved questions about her newly acquired animals, followed by Trace's condensed explanations.

"I've already grown truly fond of Lewissa," she told him between bites. "From the beginning, I felt we had a connection, you know? Like we were kindred spirits or soul mates. Is that even possible? I just love her beautiful color. And her temperament is so sweet."

Rosa came in to clear the dishes before Trace had answered all of her questions. "I've set up your dessert on the veranda, Mr. McAllister."

Hannah jumped to her feet. "Let me help with that."

Picking up the remaining items, she followed Rosa into the kitchen, the most exquisite kitchen she'd ever seen. Any discriminating chef would struggle to find fault with its lavish design and state of the art equipment.

Everything blended perfectly with the rustic architectural design prevailing throughout the home.

"Thank you, dear," Rosa said. "I hope you enjoy the blackberry shortcake. I'd like to serve champagne, too, but that's in the wine cellar, and my knees are bothering me tonight." She tilted her head. "Would you mind going down to get a bottle?"

Should she mind? Maybe. She's in the middle of nowhere with people she barely knows, and she's been asked to climb down into a dimly lit wine cellar. But paranoia was not one of her problems, so she said, "Of course not. I'm happy to help. But can't you ask Trace? I might not find the right bottle."

Her brow creased, clearly uncomfortable with Hannah's question. "Well, he can't." Rosa's voice became a whisper. "Please don't tell him I told you, but he has a problem with tight, narrow spaces. You know, claustrophobia."

Hannah whispered back. "Oh, okay. Just point me in the right direction."

Hannah carefully made her way down the steep steps into a small wine cellar. She peered at the shelves, then scanned their lengths, confused. She couldn't possibly make a mistake. Grabbing a random bottle, she climbed back into the light of the kitchen.

"All the bottles looked the same. They were all champagne."

"That is the only alcohol Mr. McAllister will drink, and he only does that on special occasions." She gave Hannah a little wink. "Just leave that here, and I'll bring it out." She pointed. "He's waiting for you on the veranda."

Leaning back in his chair, he appeared regal, confident, and undeniably handsome. Not one guy who frequented the nightclubs back in Arizona could hold a candle to this man.

He stood when she approached, then gestured for her to have a seat at the rustic, wooden table. Rosa appeared carrying a sparkling silver tray, which she set between them. The blackberry shortcake was to-die-for delicious, putting the traditional strawberry version to shame. Hannah wondered how often he had these "special occasions" and if they were ever with Callie.

Note to self: Shut up about Callie.

With champagne in hand, they stood together, watching the approaching sunset. A few swallows soared high above the rooftop in search of their last meal of the day. Within moments, the sun disappeared behind the hills, and the temperature dropped, making Hannah shiver. As if waiting for an opportunity, Trace deftly moved behind her and encircled her with his arms. Then, he rested his chin on the top of her head.

Hannah turned, needing his warmth, his strength. When she gazed into his compelling eyes, he leaned down and softly put his mouth on hers. She didn't resist. Instead, she kissed him back, her passion and desire for contact exceeding his. Encouraged, he cradled her face in his warm hands and kissed her again and again.

"Let's go inside," he whispered.

"But what about Rosa?"

"I'm pretty sure she's in her living quarters by now."

"Because that's what she always does when you have a female dinner guest?"

The ill-fated words slipped out, and her cheeks flooded with regret. Embarrassed, she bit her lip and braced herself for Trace's furious reply – one she deserved.

"No," he said, not sounding angry at all. "Because Rosa is a smart, intuitive woman. And you, pretty lady, are thinking way too much. More champagne?"

She sighed with relief. The last thing she'd wanted was to ruin this perfect evening with her sudden, ridiculous jealousy. "Yes, please. Just a little."

With their fingers linked, they went back inside. Trace guided her to a huge leather sofa facing a rock fireplace that covered a good portion of the wall. A fire had already been lit and was crackling and emitting the wonderful scent of pine.

Trace shook his head ruefully. "Rosa has outdone herself tonight." His appreciative tone was almost inaudible. "Make yourself comfortable. I'll get some fresh glasses."

Oatie had been following them around all evening, not making a sound, staying in the background, but always there. Now he lay a few feet from the fire.

"You know," she told the dog, "back in Phoenix, we never had fires in the summertime. We rarely had them in the middle of winter." She took a deep breath of the fragrant air.

Trace returned with the glasses, refilled them, and made a toast. "To you, pretty lady. What took you so long?"

What does he mean by that?

After a few more sips of the effervescent drink, they set their glasses down and kissed again. This time, the kisses came with unexpected urgency.

Suddenly, Trace pulled away, leaving her breathless. "What am I doing? I'm so sorry, Hannah. It's too soon for you." His head shook, his eyes looking down at his boots. "It's all too soon for this. Can you ever for—"

"Shh," she said and pressed her finger against his lips.

"Please, don't be sorry. I'm not. Maybe I should be, but I'm not."

Oatie whined, drawing their attention. He sat at their feet, looking up intently, as if he were their official chaperone, or was he a cheerleader? They laughed, and the dog took that joyful sound as permission to jump up on the giant sofa. After a couple of turns to make his resting spot perfect, he lay down, closed his eyes, and puffed out a contented sigh.

Trace's focus returned to Hannah. Pulling her onto his lap, he picked up where they'd left off. "Pardon my dog," he said between kisses. "This is a new experience for him."

"Really?" she murmured. "It's new for me too."

She'd kissed a few men – two, to be exact – but those kisses never felt like this. Being kissed by this powerful, magnificent man was like living in a fairy tale, except that the handsome prince was a cowboy, and the castle was a giant log home. Tonight she felt certain that Trace's mouth was created for the sole purpose of kissing her, but what would tomorrow bring?

SEVEN

Hannah awoke, slowly letting her mind adjust to the shuffling sounds of horses in the corral and to the persistent squawking of chickens. She was pretty sure several upset squirrels were adding to the ruckus. The sun beamed through an open window as she recalled last night's glorious sunset, the fireplace, the champagne, and Trace's warm arms and sizzling kisses.

It had been close to midnight when he drove her home. Holding hands, they'd walked up the steps together. He seemed as hungry for her as she was for him, but after one long, delicious kiss, he said goodnight. Remembering that kiss brought a smile to her face and tingles of desire a bit lower.

But today was a new day. *Rise and shine!* Morning

came early on a ranch, she'd learned. Throwing on her only jeans and zipping up her only sweatshirt – she was in desperate need of a serious shopping day – she strolled outside to greet and feed her animals.

The horses seemed agitated, especially Lewissa. Even the chickens showed concern, stretching their necks like giraffes while standing perfectly still. *Was that a bad sign?* What did they know that she did not? Curious, Hannah peered around the ranch and spotted a car hesitating at the far end of her driveway. Before she got a good look, it turned back onto the dirt road and was out of sight. A lost traveler using the driveway to turn around, she assumed, then concluded that her animals didn't take well to strangers on the property; she liked that.

Turning back to those animals, she scattered feed for the chickens and flakes of alfalfa and hay for the horses. Trace had assured her there was no need to supplement the cows yet. Plenty of green grass still waved in the pasture. *If only the Phoenix partying crowd could see me now.* Imagining their shocked expressions put a smile on her face, but that smile was short-lived.

Thinking about them brought up an image of Rick and his untimely, fiery death. She could only hope it had come quickly, that he hadn't suffered. Selfishly, she admitted that it was a good thing she hadn't been in love or sexually involved with him. That was a definite plus for her, but she could find no bright side to any of this for Rick. Death had no silver lining.

What would it feel like to lose a man I truly loved? She hoped to never find out.

For the past three years, she'd led an ordinary life consumed with waitressing all week and dancing with Rick on the weekends. Nothing serious. Nothing complicated. Losing someone she loved was a foreign concept to her. She had no experience to draw from, thank goodness, except for the love she felt for her mother, but that was different. And her mother was alive.

Hannah looked up when Lewissa nudged her shoulder and huffed out a warm, moist breath.

"I'm all right. Just having a brief mental setback," she assured the horse, offering a piece of peppermint candy from her pants pocket and then taking one for herself. Lewissa liked the sweet treat and crunched it loudly. "I'm feeling much better about living on the ranch with you by my side, and with Trace less than twenty miles to the north."

She felt a little trapped, though. Staying here without a vehicle was impossible, so she added *Buy a Car* to her list of tasks. Having lived her entire life as a lower-middle-class citizen, she was a bargain hunter, a good one. A small, used truck would do. Then she could pick up the animals' food and be self-sufficient on the ranch.

She had to make a go of her new life. If she didn't, she might end up like her mom: Unsettled, unfulfilled, and lonely. *I miss my mom.*

Back inside, she settled on the loveseat and powered up her laptop for the first time since her arrival. She didn't expect to find many car and truck dealers in the small town, but there had to be at least one. She wasn't finicky when it came to modes of transportation. She clicked on the browser icon, typed *car dealerships,* and waited impatiently for the results. After a second or two, a message popped up: *No Connection! Check your WiFi Settings and Try Again.* Hannah rolled her eyes, exasperated. No Internet access. *Ugh! I've been transported back to the dark ages!*

After a bit of fussing, Hannah came to terms with the technical limitations and delays that stood in her way. She shifted her thinking to the banking task that needed attention. It shouldn't be difficult. A simple online transfer of the funds from Rick's account to hers was all she had to do. She had the necessary passwords. *Darn!* That transaction also required an Internet connection.

Surrendering to the temporary stumbling blocks, she grabbed a cold soda, then stood by the north-facing window watching the livestock. Her small herd of cows seemed content, taking slow, lazy steps as they grazed on the healthy green grass. *Someday, I will be content.*

She needed to do something, but she wasn't sure what. She had no job to dash off to, no need to prepare for a night of dancing, karaoke, and fun. That's when the *aha* moment hit her. *Do what I came here to do!*

She grabbed one of her drawing pads and a 4H graphite pencil, which she carried to the bench closest to the corral. Lewissa proved to be an excellent model. Other than some horse-talk with her head and mouth, she stood perfectly still. Before thirty minutes had passed, Hannah had completed her first Colorado drawing.

"Thank you, Lewissa," she said and was about to give her one more treat, but it slipped from her hand, bounced off the corral panel and onto the ground. No big deal. As she reached for it, something shiny caught her eye. "My locket! I've been looking everywhere for it." Picking it up, she brushed off the dirt and vowed to wear it only on special occasions from now on.

"Okay, Lewissa, let's try this again. She rewarded the horse with another peppermint candy and a nose rub. "This may be my best drawing ever." She wondered if a horse could be a muse.

Lewissa nodded, then wiggled her lips, showing her teeth as if she were smiling. Hannah laughed. She thought her horse was a smart, beautiful animal from day one, but today she got a glimpse of her comical side. A horse with a sense of humor. Was that possible?

Thinking clearly and feeling refreshed, Hannah went back inside and headed straight to the phone. She didn't need to wait for the Internet. She could accomplish the bank transfer with a simple phone call.

The voice on the other end was all business. "I'm sorry, ma'am, but I am not able to speak with you about an account which does not bear your name."

"Are you sure about that? I thought it did." Hannah hesitated. "I was there when Rick and I opened the account. I have the account number, the online login, and the password. Doesn't that count for something?"

"I'm afraid not. If it's any consolation, that account was closed three days ago."

What? Why would Rick have closed the account?

Wait! That's impossible.

"You must be mistaken. Four days ago, Rick died in a terrible car accident in Colorado. So you see, he could not have closed our account three days ago. Please, can you double-check your facts?"

"There is no mistake, ma'am. I'm looking at the account as we speak. Your friend, Mr. Johnson, closed the account three days ago just like I said."

Hannah's heartbeat pounded in her temples, and perspiration broke out along her hairline. "H-how much was in the account when he closed it?"

"I can't give you that information, either. Only the account holder can—"

"But the account holder is dead! And that was my money!" Tears of confusion filled her eyes. *How can this be happening?* "I need to speak with the bank manager. I met him the day we made the original deposit."

"Certainly. I'll see if he's in."

Surely someone had made mistakes – big ones. Annoying background music played in Hannah's ear as she waited – it seemed like forever – for the manager. She doubted that many of this bank's clients had accounts with balances as high as this one. Perhaps they were trying to fix their mistake before continuing this conversation. That could explain the long wait time.

"Mr. Maxwell, here," she eventually heard. "I understand you're trying to withdraw money from an account that isn't yours and no longer exists."

I've gone from living in the dark ages to being trapped in the twilight zone.

Ignoring his unhelpful, sarcastic statement, Hannah pushed forward. "I *know* you did not just hand over that much cash to some stranger. Was it a check or a bank transfer?"

"We are not able to give out that or any information to anyone but the account holder. I'm sure you can understand that," he said in a condescending tone.

"And I am sure you must remember the day when Rick and I met with you and made that large deposit. I believe we also spoke with you about the adventure we were planning."

Mr. Maxwell's impatient sigh traveled over the phone line loud and clear. "Might I suggest you get in touch with the account holder and a lawyer?"

Hannah, beside herself, responded with angry sobs. "Rick. Is. Dead. Don't you get it?"

"That may be, but the bank has no record of that. If you could submit the official death certificate and if he had a will, we might be able to help you." The banker paused. "What I will tell you, ma'am – and because this was such an uncommon, large transaction, I do remember it well – is that the same man who opened the account closed it. I assure you he had all the proper identification and was very much alive."

The phone slipped from Hannah's numb hand.

WHEN TRACE WALKED IN, he saw Hannah sitting on the loveseat, shaking like an aspen leaf in October. She seemed more upset today than when the sheriff delivered the news of her friend's death.

"Hannah? You okay? I knocked, but when you didn't

answer, I took the liberty of entering. I didn't mean to scare you." He sat next to her and reached for her hand. It was cold and slick with perspiration. "I came by to make sure last night wasn't just a dream. And also to check on Lewissa."

By now, Oatie's front half was in Hannah's lap, but she didn't seem to notice. When the dog whined, her hand didn't pat his head or scratch his ears.

Trace looked on, concern hardening in his chest. "Are you having second thoughts or regrets about last night?"

Still, no reaction.

"Come on, sweetie, talk to me."

He observed her as she inhaled deeply. Even so, her words came out in a shaky whisper.

"There's no Internet here. No WiFi."

"Yeah," he said, thinking about his reply. "It's kind of like the electricity and the phone. It has to be turned on and, in this case, installed. To the best of my knowledge, there's never been a satellite dish here."

She stared straight ahead. Had she heard him? This was frustrating. He'd always known he was far more skilled with horses than he was with women, but her reaction to the lack of an Internet connection was way over the top.

"I'll call our local satellite company right now. Would that make you feel better?"

All he got was a nod. He helped himself to a can of soda, took a swallow, and gave the rest to Hannah. While he made the call, he noticed she'd begun to pet Oatie and sip the soda. That was a good sign.

"An installer will be here in a day or two," he said, hanging up. "Then you'll be online. If there's something that can't wait, you're welcome to come over to my place. My Internet connection works well, except in a snowstorm."

"Thank you. I appreciate your kindness."

Neither her mood nor her expression had lightened, even with the good news. Trace was at a loss.

"Tell me what's going on, Hannah." He tipped her chin up gently, and their eyes met. "Talk to me. I want to help."

She sighed, then shared her mystifying story.

"Let me get this straight," Trace eventually said, leaning back. "You won the lottery and handed half of your winnings over to Rick?"

"Yes, in a way. He'd asked if I'd meant what I said about wanting to start a new life that included outdoor adventure as well as a time and a place where I could be an artist. He suggested that he hold onto half of my money so that he could take care of all the arrangements."

Trace fought the urge to punch his fist through the nearest wall. How could she have been so naïve?

Her crazy story rolled around in his head, but the fact that Rick had withdrawn the money after his own death was a hell of a lot crazier. The facts didn't add up.

"Hannah, how much money did you win?"

"After taxes," her head tilted slightly, and her eyes looked upward, "almost five million."

"Holy shit!"

EIGHT

Hannah insisted that the bank had made a mistake. She went so far as to suggest that someone there had stolen the money, or there had been a cyber-attack on the account.

"Those are all possibilities, but highly unlikely," Trace said, mixing concern with logic. It seemed Hannah had considered every reason except the obvious one – that Rick had faked his own death and was now alive and extremely rich.

"Hannah, some people would do just about anything to get their hands on that kind of money. *Anything*."

She stared at him, wide-eyed. "I know what you're thinking. If Rick drained the bank account, that would mean he's not dead, and he stole my money. But then who died in our Range Rover?"

Trace waited, wondering if she'd come to the same conclusion he had. He did not want to be the one to bring it up.

"Oh my God!" she whispered, suddenly pale. "Did Rick murder someone?"

"I don't know."

He wrapped his arms around her waist and pulled her close. She trembled, and he understood exactly why. If Rick *was* a murderer, Hannah's good friend had become a dangerous man. *Maybe he'd always been a bad guy.* This new possibility changed the direction of his thinking. Now he was more determined than ever to keep her safe if it was the last thing he did.

Trace's ranch phone rang. "Dad, what a surprise." The conversation was brief and left him frowning, feeling torn.

"Is everything all right?" Hannah asked, leading him to the sofa and climbing onto his lap.

"You have the prettiest green eyes I've ever seen," said Trace, changing the subject.

"Thank you. I thought they seemed a little greener lately. Must be the reflection of all the greenness here at the ranch." She kissed the corner of his mouth softly.

Unable to resist, he kissed her back. "You know what they say about green eyes, don't you?" he asked, catching his breath.

"No, I don't know what they say about green eyes. You do?"

"Yep. I do."

"And just how did you acquire such uncommon knowledge?"

"From my mother."

"Don't keep me in suspense. I need details."

He kissed her lightly on her smiling and warm lips. "If you insist," he said, adding a kiss on the tip of her nose. "People with eyes as green as yours are rare. They're usually curious, quick-witted, caring, and intuitive."

"Hmm. And how does your mother know that?"

"Let's just say you and my mother have something in common." He frowned again, knowing what words he'd say next. "Speaking of mothers, I've got to make a quick trip to Denver. She's not feeling well and has requested my presence."

He saw the disappointment in her eyes and wanted to comfort her, but he also wanted to grin. How wonderful to know she'd miss him.

"And now you need to let me up," he said, smiling innocently.

"You're leaving right this minute?"

"I want to check on Lewissa. I promise I'll be right back."

He and Oatie went to the corral. He gave each horse a quick neck rub and then turned his back to the house and made a phone call.

"We're back, and I'm hungry. How about you?"

"I could eat something, but our choices are sorry limited. I have to tell you, the selection of meal-making ingredients brought by your grocery delivery service provided few options, nothing deserving of praise. But I'll whip something up."

It didn't matter to Trace what she made. He wasn't hungry. He just needed to stall and keep her from thinking too much right now.

"Hey, whatever you're making smells downright good enough to eat."

"It should. It's an old family recipe," she said, knowing full well there was no such thing.

When he raised his brows, a mischievous grin spread across her sweet face as she set, with great ceremony, a cup of her concoction in front of him.

"You are enjoying a can of vegetable soup combined with a can of corn and broken bits of pasta. Oh, and I put some canned meat in yours." Her nose wrinkled, and she shuddered at the thought.

"It's good. Really."

When they'd finished, he pulled her toward him and held her. Just held her. The thought of going to Denver did not sit well in his gut. He didn't want to leave her alone. Not even for a day. She smiled, then reached up and wrapped her arms around his neck.

"Hannah," he said, "I'm glad you're here at the ranch. Holding you does my heart good." He thought about mentioning that it also did his body good, but she likely already knew that.

She stiffened. "I hear something. A car? I hope it's not the sheriff."

"It's Rosa."

"And she's here, because…?"

"I asked her to bring you one of our small pickups to use until you get your own." Hannah's expression changed, but he was unable to interpret its meaning. "I'll feel better knowing you have transportation while I'm gone."

He handed her a key from his key ring, wrote down his city cell number again, then gave her a long, warm hug. He put his nose in her soft, silky hair and breathed in, her sweet scent causing his heart to skip a beat. Then, slowly, he let her go, but just before heading out the door to Rosa, he looked down at Oatie and told him to stay.

"One more thing," he called out from his truck as Rosa climbed into the passenger seat beside him. "Phone me, even if you have nothing to say." He grinned because most of the time she had plenty to say. "If I don't hear from you, I'll worry. Got it?"

She ran out of the house and stood on tiptoe by the truck's window. When he leaned out, she pressed her lips against his.

"Got it!" she said.

He drove away slowly, watching her as long as he could with the help of his rearview mirror. His brain had teamed up with his gut, each nagging fiercely: Don't leave her alone. *But Mother needs me too.* Typically, his mother was strong and selfless; she rarely asked for anything. Today was an exception. She'd specifically asked for him to come, and he couldn't disappoint her. What had his dad called it? *Something medical.*

"Oh, hell!" The only feasible plan? To take care of everything, fast. He'd drop Rosa back at the ranch, go straight to Denver and check on his mother, then return to Hannah ASAP. Still, something didn't feel right.

THE PICKUP WAS small compared to the truck Trace drove. Even so, it was bigger than the car she had back in Phoenix. She placed a pillow on the seat so she could see over the top of the steering wheel. As she turned the key, she glanced at the passenger seat, making sure she had everything: purse, credit card, and shopping list.

She was about to pull away when she saw Oatie sitting on the porch watching her. What should she do with him? She couldn't risk losing Trace's best friend, so she ran back and put him in the house along with a bowl of water.

"I'll be back in a few hours, Oatie. You guard the house, okay?" she scratched his ears and made a mental note to buy dog food and a few treats.

At the end of the driveway, she hesitated, knowing that a left turn would take her to town and a right turn to Trace's ranch. She sighed. Today was a left turn day.

There wasn't much to the town. The one main street – aptly named Main Street – was about eight blocks long. At one end stood a Farm & Feed Store, a Kmart Super Store was at the other. Between the two, she noticed a Healthfood Unlimited, a hardware store, a beauty shop, a few restaurants, and even a tiny movie theater.

Once inside Kmart, she could have been in Anytown, USA. They were all arranged the same and looked the same, except that many Native Americans shopped at this store. She enjoyed watching the families fill their baskets. Her own basket, not even half full, contained everything she currently needed.

On the drive back to her ranch, she was content

knowing the truck carried fresh fruits and vegetables, eggs, tofu, two bottles of wine, a bag of dark chocolate squares, coffee, and some Styrofoam cups. She'd also purchased three picture frames, including matting and backing, as well as a few more graphite drawing pencils and charcoal sticks.

Oatie had his own bag, filled with food, treats, and a tennis ball. She'd needed a few items of clothing and was pleased with her purchase of two pair of jeans, some pretty t-shirts, boots to wear around the ranch, a pink hoodie, and a jean jacket. Last but not least, though not without hesitation, she'd selected three sets of panties and bras (pale pink, baby blue, and black lace) and one white, silky teddy for sleeping on warm nights. That's what she told herself.

Poised on her pillow and with the engine running smoothly, she smiled, pleased with her first venture into the small, country town – all by herself. However, her cheerful mood disappeared in an instant when she spotted The Pizza Place at the side of the road. Rick's final destination.

What happened between the time he'd left their ranch to pick up a pizza and the moment the Range Rover veered off the road? That thought led to additional wondering. What happened to the two million dollars they'd deposited in the bank? She doubted the ranch cost that much, but she really did not know. Rick handled all of that.

Her thoughts, these questions, began to unfold like an unfortunate, senseless mystery. As much as she enjoyed reading and watching them on TV, she'd never wanted to be part of one, especially one that involved the death of a friend – or was it the death of a stranger? Either way, she'd not signed up for anything deadly.

About a half-mile from home, she noticed an ordinary gray sedan parked off to the side of the dirt road. The vehicle appeared to be empty. A shiver rippled down her spine.

"Stop that," she said out loud, remembering that a small river meandered just down the hill. "Probably a fisherman."

Then, the site of an unfamiliar van parked by her house almost sent her racing back to town, but she drove closer anyway. With relief, she read the words *Blue Moon Satellite Installation* painted on its side.

Oatie was doing his job, barking furiously at the man waiting by the front door.

"Hello," she called. "I'll be right there."

Grabbing the bag filled with items needing refrigeration, she hurried toward the door. Oatie barked and growled, refusing to calm down, as Hannah put the key in the lock. The installer wore ill-fitting clothing and had a horrible haircut. Even the color of his hair looked awful. It was as if he were dressed up for Halloween, trying to look like Wayne Newton in desperate need of a shave. Maybe he knew how awful he looked, and that was why he kept his sunglasses on even after they went inside.

"Sorry about the dog," she said. "I'm watching him for a friend. I could keep him outside while you do your installation. I need to feed the horses anyway."

"Sure. Take the dog. I'm just looking for existing wiring and possible locations for your dish. I'll be out of your hair in fifteen minutes."

"Oh, okay. Holler if you need anything."

Almost thirty minutes had passed, and the installer had not yet come out. Hannah headed back inside, hoping there wasn't a problem. Access to the Internet was her primary connection to the outside world. She could live without TV; DVDs were fine in a pinch, but the Internet? She had to have it.

She found Mr. Ugly Satellite Man hunched over in her bedroom closet. Weird. "Is there a problem?"

"Uh, nope. I think we're good to go for tomorrow's installation. Just keep that dog away from me."

She shrugged. "He's a great dog. Sorry he didn't take to you better."

In truth, Hannah hadn't taken to the man much better than Oatie had. Something about him made her uncomfortable. Though she desperately wanted Internet service, she wasn't looking forward to seeing him again.

Her treasure trove of food, clothing, art pencils, and picture frames beckoned, so she set to work unpacking. Oatie chowed down noisily, keeping an eye on Hannah as he ate. Standing at the kitchen counter, she placed the photo of her mom in one of the new frames, then did the same for Rick's photo and her new drawing of Lewissa. She wanted to make certain that the glass was spotless and the matting straight. She'd even purchased upgraded cardboard, paper, and frame clamps for the backing because more than memories would be stored within these frames.

Pleased with her workmanship and color choices for the matting, the three frames were ready to be displayed. She chose the mantel above the fireplace, but when she picked up the frames and took a step back from the counter, the dog yelped, and she nearly fell.

"Whoa! Oatie! What are you doing there?"

Apparently, after finishing his meal, he'd settled down directly behind her. Her affection for him grew with each second they spent together. She never had a dog of her own, never knew what she'd been missing until now.

"I'm so sorry! I almost squashed you." His tail whipped around in forgiving circles. "You know what? If you were mine, I'd have named you Velcro because of how well you are sticking by me."

Scrutinizing the mantel, she decided to place Mom's photo to the left, Rick's to the right, and Lewissa's drawing in the center. Still admiring her first bit of home decorating, she jumped when the phone rang, then rushed to answer it, hoping it was Trace.

"Could I speak with Ms. Hannah?"

"Yes, that's me."

An awkward silence followed, punctuated by a few *uhs* and *hmms*. "I'm so sorry about today," he said.

"What? Who is this?"

The man cleared his throat. "My name is Ross. I'm the owner of Blue Moon Satellite Installation. I just wanted to apologize for the no-show today. That has never happened before. We take pride in giving our customers excellent and personal service. An installer will be there tomorrow morning for sure."

Confused, her heart skipped. "But he *was* here today."

"No, ma'am. My guy never made it to your place. There was – a problem. But we'll make it up to you with a few extra GBs this first month."

She couldn't speak.

"Ma'am? Are you still there?"

She hung up and plopped down onto the sofa, stunned. Oatie leaped up from his position on the floor and sat with her. He pawed her arm and stared intently into her eyes as if he were trying to send her a message. She nodded her understanding and gave the dog a hug.

"I know, Oatie, I know. You were right about that creepy guy," said Hannah, still holding on to him. "I'm so lucky you were here, but we have to tell Trace." Running her hand over Oatie's back, she slowly let go and reached for the phone.

"Trace?"

NINE

Trace heard the tension, the fear in Hannah's voice when she'd called. Everything he knew about fight or flight and predator/prey pertained to horses, but he easily transferred those concepts to Hannah. If a predator was lurking nearby, she was the prey. The natural instinct for any prey was to flee the danger or fight when given no other option. What would this slender, gentle woman do? She didn't have a violent bone in her body.

Hannah and Oatie met Trace at the door. Despite the late hour, her eyes were wide-open, though she looked exhausted. The dog, after a brief, energetic greeting, curled up and went back to sleep.

"I'm sorry," she said, sounding embarrassed. "You didn't need to leave your mother in such a hurry."

He wrapped his arms around her and kissed the top of her head. "Yes, I did. I'm glad you called. I don't know what's going on or if any connections exist between these strange events, but it's all troubling, and you shouldn't be alone. Besides, Mother insisted I get back to you right away, and she's the wisest woman I know."

"Does that mean your mother is going to be all right?"

He stalled, not having a good answer. "Knowing her, she'd say everything was fine whether it was or not. She'll have a thorough checkup per doctor's orders, and a battery of tests will begin in the morning."

"She sounds like a strong woman."

Trace nodded, but he knew being strong didn't fix everything. He informed Hannah that he'd be spending the rest of the night sleeping on her couch. She didn't object. He tucked her into bed and leaned down to kiss her on the forehead. Oatie jumped up, nudged him aside, and curled into a ball beside her.

"Is that okay with you, Hannah? Oatie sleeping on the bed?" He eyed the dog skeptically. "He doesn't do that at home."

"He seems to like it."

I'll bet he does.

AT DAWN, Trace opened his eyes and blinked, thinking he must be dreaming. Hannah lay on the short couch, just beyond his reach, wearing one of those little, silky, pajama things. *How am I supposed to control my heart... and everything else*, he thought.

Oatie lay on the floor between them, keeping one eye open. The woodstove still emitted a slight glow and an ounce of warmth.

Shifting quietly from his back to his side and his head supported by one arm, Trace settled in to enjoy the magnificent view. Long, fair hair tumbled around her shoulders, though a couple of strands curled gently over her beautiful, tranquil face. She looked like a sleeping angel.

The phone rang, its unexpected sound jarring. Hannah sprang to her feet and hurried to answer it. Trace followed right behind her, concerned that it might be the hospital calling. He'd given his dad this number, just in case. He stood by her side as she answered, trying to read her expression. There was no mistaking her anger. Her mouth drew tight, her eyes ablaze. Anger at dawn? Not good.

"Yes. He's here," Hannah snapped. He hadn't heard that tone from her sweet mouth before, nor had he been given that particular look. "It's Callie, calling from *your* place."

What a relief. It wasn't the hospital. "Oh, thank God."

If looks could kill, he'd be dead. After a rapid exit from the room, Hannah returned wearing jeans and a sweatshirt, then headed directly outside toward the horse corral, not giving him another glance.

After a quick conversation with Callie, he hung up the phone and followed her out. "What's the matter?"

"Oh, I don't know," she replied, her tone feigning sweetness. "What could possibly be the matter with me? Callie calls you from your house before sunrise, and you seem pleased, almost happy. Should I go on? I don't need to be a math wiz to put two and two together."

Where had *that* come from? Trace shook his head. "And I don't need to be a psychiatric genius to know that your interpretation is seriously flawed." Before he could continue, his own phone buzzed. It was Rosa with additional information. "Dammit! There's a big problem at the ranch. I've got to go."

IF THE INSTALLER hadn't showed up at 9:15 a.m., she'd still be wondering who to be mad at. Callie, Trace, or herself. But there he was, the real installer at her door. He completed the job in forty-five minutes.

When Hannah asked him about the *other* installer, he appeared confused.

"This is a real small company, ma'am. What you see is what you get," he said, jabbing one thumb at his chest. That was all he was willing to say though he had to know more. Much more.

No doubt about it. Yesterday's guy had been an imposter. What had he wanted? After the authentic installer left, she went through her meager belongings, but nothing was missing. *Why had he been here?* That question lingered in her thoughts the rest of the day.

Hannah had almost finished creating a Facebook account when she heard the sound of Trace's truck approaching. Nerves of anticipation danced through her chest. Every conversation they'd had so far had been either wonderful or awful. She wasn't up to any more *awful*.

No matter what he said, she resolved to do everything in her power to remain sweet and helpful. He had problems too – his mother in the hospital and some kind of complication at the ranch early this morning – and she needed to keep that in mind.

She went to the window and watched him step from the truck. Then, as if under a magical spell, she could not look away. His stride was easy and confident, not an average man's walk. He resembled a leading man in a modern-day western movie. And here he was, this cowboy with star quality, returning to her.

Oatie barked, bringing her back to the moment and her relentless suspicions. Perhaps he'd come only to get his dog. Anxious to see him, but full of apprehension and doubt from their talk earlier that day, she walked to the door and opened it just as he strode up the stairs.

Trace stood outside the door, covered in mud. He removed his cowboy hat and held it at his side. "Hi. Can we talk?"

"Yes. I think we should."

He asked Hannah to follow him to the bench by the corral. Lewissa trotted over, passing Trace and nuzzling up to Hannah. She tickled the horse under its chin and offered one of the peppermint treats she always kept in her pocket now. On any other day, knowing that she and her horse loved the same sweet treat would have brought a smile to her face. But not today. Not until she heard what Trace had to say.

She joined him on the bench, noting the uncomfortable vacant space between them.

"What was the problem at the ranch?" *Did I really want to know?*

He shook his head, obviously not happy. "One of the cows from the southern pasture turned up dead. Fortunately, Callie recognized the symptoms – sorry, Hannah, but the girl really does know cows – and she called me right away. Seems the cow was poisoned, so we checked everything out and determined the stock tank was the source. Someone had put poison in the water. If I hadn't gotten there when I did, a lot more cows would have died."

Hannah's jaw dropped. "Who would do such a thing? Do you have enemies?"

"Not that I know of, but I guess I do. I can't afford to be tied up with cow-sitting right now, and I can't pull the hands from the northern pasture. Their plates are already piled high. I'll need to hire an extra hand, a nighthawk, to watch over the herd."

They sat quietly on the bench. Even the comical clucking of chickens did little to ease the tension between them. Hannah made the first move, scooting closer to Trace. He still looked straight ahead, deep in thought, but he took her hand and kissed her fingertips. Relief flowed through her. His presence gave her a new kind of strength, grit, and courage – *country* courage.

"What's next?" she asked quietly. "What should we do? It seems like we now have at least three puzzles to solve."

"Three?"

Had he not been counting? Or were there *more* than three on his list?

"That's what I've come up with." She held up one finger. "The missing money withdrawn from the bank by Rick – who is supposed to be a dead man." A second finger lifted. "A creepy, snooping, fake satellite dish installer. And now, a cow killer is lurking about. That's three."

He nodded, but his eyes had changed. "You know what I think?" In one smooth move, he took her face in his hands, and his lips touched hers, sending tingles through her body. "I think we need a day off for a little R&R. What do you say?"

What *could* she say? She was hypnotized by his spell. "What do you suggest?"

His chin rose, indicating Lewissa. "These horses need to get out of the corral. Let's take them for a ride tomorrow. I'll have Rosa pack a picnic."

Hannah hesitated. She'd never sat on a real horse before. Riding a wooden merry-go-round horse as a little girl was as close as she'd come, and that made her dizzy. She assumed riding a real horse might be trickier. What if she fell off? Or worse, what if she looked incompetent and foolish?

"We'll just walk the horses," he assured her, likely noting her concern. "No trotting or galloping. What do you say?"

She eyed him warily. "Just the two of us, right?"

"Yeah, of course. Who else would I bring along?"

"Oh, I don't know. Maybe Miss Callie, your cowgirl." She flinched, immediately regretting the insinuation. That was no way to move forward.

"I'm going to ignore that comment for now," he said, lifting an eyebrow with a teasing frown. Standing up, he stepped heavily toward Lewissa and Clark, who stood together at the corral's far end. Clark shifted to welcome him. Lewissa, on the other hand, shied away and wandered back to Hannah.

"It seems we have another issue to deal with," he called out as he, too, walked toward Hannah. "Are you jealous?"

With a slight hesitation, she said, "Maybe, a little."

"Well, then. That makes two of us."

What? Confused, she spotted a teasing glint in his eye. "You're jealous of Callie too?" she asked.

He grinned. "Nope. I'm a little envious – call it jealous, if you want – of your relationship with Lewissa. She prefers your company to mine. That has never happened before, and I'm the experienced horse person. Do you have any idea how that makes me feel?"

"No." Lewissa pressed her warm muzzle to Hannah's cheek, her ears flicking as Hannah murmured to her.

"Huh." He stopped in front of her and looked down, his eyes warm. "She's usually not so mellow. How do you do that? It's like you speak with her, telepathically."

Hannah shrugged. "I don't know about that. I think it's more like positive thinking. I focus strongly on something I want her to know, and I imagine that she understands my thoughts or feelings. It doesn't always work."

"The power of positive thinking?" He looked skeptical. "Well, whatever it is, it's interesting." He gave her that confident smile, lifting the weight from her heart. "Listen, can we stop this discussion and move on for now? We can get back to our puzzles and personal issues tomorrow, right after our picnic. Okay with you?"

How could she argue? All she wanted was to be with him.

"Oh, and by the way, you may not be a cowgirl yet, but you're the loveliest woman I've ever seen, and I have a feeling you will be the best *horse-woman* in a very short time."

Trace's compliment made her day. "Do you have a minute to walk with me to the lower pasture? I was hoping you could teach me more about the cows before you head out. Also, I have a question about Buttercup's horns."

"Buttercup?" He looked concerned. "You've named the cows?"

"Not all of them… yet. I'll give each a name when a perfect one pops up."

Trace scratched his head. "You do know the fate of most beef cattle, right?"

She did *not* want to think about that. She put her hands on her hips and glared up at him. "Listen to yourself. The defining keyword, Mr. Rancher, was 'most,' not *all*. My cows won't end up that way."

"You're way out in left field here. You're in cattle ranch territory. Surely you know that." She nodded, and he shook his head with wonder. "Sometimes I don't understand you."

"Ditto," she said, lifting her chin a little higher. She sensed the sarcasm building, threatening to burst out, but managed to keep it under wraps. "I happen to love my cows."

Trace turned and stomped toward the truck, insisting that Oatie come with him. He looked back at Hannah, then called out a few parting words. "Just don't get too attached to them. That's all I'm trying to say."

She waited until his truck was gone, then let the tears stream down her cheeks. Feeling completely out of control, she ran non-stop to the lower pasture. There, she searched her mind for a perfect name for each nameless cow.

THE STILETTOS, THE CABIN, & THE CURSE

TEN

Should he call her? Or should he wait for her to call him? It was late by the time he allowed himself to give in and make the call. Dammit! Her line buzzed with a busy signal.

He attempted to pass the time writing paychecks for Rosa, Callie, and the four ranch hands. Even so, he couldn't concentrate. Denying the truth only made matters worse. He was drawn to Hannah like a bear to honey, waiting for the sting.

He wondered if the recent stress could be the cause of her irrational words and actions. Every time he tried to put himself in her shoes, he failed miserably. He was certain of one thing, though. Ever since their first kiss, life had become a little too mystifying.

He called again. Still busy. Who could Hannah be

talking to for so long at this late hour? Or had she taken her phone off the hook to avoid speaking with him? He wasn't sure he wanted to know the answer. An unexpected knock at his den's door derailed his frustrating train of thought.

Before he could say "come in," there stood Callie, dressed in uptown clothing, a far cry from her usual small town, Daisy Duke style. For Trace to notice a gal's wardrobe, the change had to be radical, and this change fit that bill.

"Where've you been, Callie? Does your mother know you've been out and about this late?"

"Hey, I'm gonna be nineteen in a few months. I'm an adult, in case ya hadn't noticed. I can do whatever I want, whenever I want."

"Suit yourself. Just don't do anything you wouldn't want her to know about 'cause we talk." His eyes returned to the work on his desk.

"Fine. Whatever you say, boss."

After a moment's reflection, he decided to ask his question again. "No, really. Where have you been? Thought you were going to stay in the small bunkhouse until I hired a replacement for Frank."

"That's where I've been sleeping, and that's where I'll sleep tonight unless I get a better offer." She slinked closer to him, sat on his desk, and batted her long lashes.

"I finished my work and had a couple of errands to run for a friend. I don't see what the big deal is."

Callie had no limits, but she did have persistence. She stepped behind Trace and began to rub his neck. He was so tired. He closed his eyes briefly, imagining Hannah's hands until they ventured under his shirt.

"Cut it out, Callie. I've got work to do."

She gave him a finger-wiggling wave, then turned and strutted toward the door. With amazement, he watched her long legs walk across the room, her feet in incredibly high heels. How did she walk in those things? Her mother was right; Callie was trouble.

Hannah's phone was still busy. His gut told him something was wrong. Should he go to her and risk looking like a blundering idiot? The problem could be as simple as the phone being off the hook. But if that was it, how had it gotten that way? He needed to find out. After that, he'd see if they could patch up today's little tiff. Yeah, he'd take the risk.

He pulled away from his ranch and headed south. He drove too fast and prayed that no wildlife jumped onto the road in front of him. From experience, he knew he wouldn't be able to stop in time. Eventually, he made the turn into her driveway and slowed down. He expected darkness at this time of night, but light glowed from several windows. That canceled his falling-asleep-with-the-phone-off-the-hook theory.

He was surprised to see Lewissa prancing around the corral in the dark, obviously agitated. *Mountain lion? Coyotes?*

Oatie beat him up the steps and was now barking for Hannah's attention. When she opened the door, Trace was shocked by her appearance. She was wrapped in a blanket, her eyes puffy and red. Coming from an all-male family – except for his strong, independent mother – he'd never learned how to handle an upset woman. Still, here he was, face-to-face with a woman in distress – one he cared about – as uncomfortable, helpless feelings swirled deep in his gut.

"I thought you'd call." Her words were little more than a whisper, and she hiccupped a sob. "I kept waiting, and when you didn't—"

He took a breath, relieved to see that nothing terrible had happened. "But I did call. A dozen times." Before she could object, he swept her off her feet and carried her over to the couch. Setting her down gently, he knelt and took her cold hands in his. "Every time I called, I got a busy signal." He brushed a silky strand of hair from her eyes.

She had only one phone, and he found the handset sitting firmly on its base. He'd learned in his thirty years of life that often the simplest answer was the right answer. Curious, he picked up the phone and put it to his ear. He heard nothing. The phone was dead.

"Wait here. You, too, Oatie. I want to check something outside."

Heading down the porch steps, he went to his truck and grabbed a large flashlight. He circled the house, looking for the exterior cables. He soon found the problem and decided he'd call the phone company first thing in the morning.

Before going back inside, he stopped by the corral to check on Lewissa. If she had been a human, he reckoned he'd call her behavior tonight pacing. "Easy girl. What's going on?" The horse kept looking toward the house, nodding her head nervously. "You want Hannah, don't you? All right. I'll see if she's available."

Trace made one more trip back to the truck, grabbed his handgun, and tucked it under his belt.

Hannah looked up as Trace entered. Oatie snuggled close at her side. "Is the phone broken already?"

"Your phone is fine. There's a problem with the cable. We'll get it fixed in the morning." He didn't want to tell her that someone had been here – after he'd left in a huff over a stupid argument about cow naming – and that someone had cut her phone cables.

"I think your horse wants to see you," he said, trying to cheer her up. "Do you mind coming outside?"

"Of course not." Looking energized, she tossed the blanket on the sofa and tugged her old sweatshirt over her head. "Let's go."

The minute Hannah stepped outside, Lewissa stopped her pacing and trotted in her direction. The scene was impressive, even to a horse expert like himself. The gal definitely had a gift when it came to communicating with this animal, or was it the other way around?

"Lewissa, tomorrow you're going to take me for a ride," Hannah said quietly. The horse's soft ears twitched, listening. "You will have to be extra gentle because I've never ridden a horse before."

Lewissa whinnied her approval and shook her mane, the previous tension all gone. Together, Trace, Hannah, and Oatie walked back to the house.

"Does that mean our picnic is still on?"

She glanced shyly at him. "I guess it does."

He hesitated before making his next request – actually, it was a demand – and he wasn't about to take 'no' for an answer.

"I'm staying here with you tonight," he informed her. He didn't want to leave her alone ever again. "Rosa can drop off our picnic lunch on her way to town. After that, we'll ride out."

With the sky dark and the hour late, he made himself comfortable on the couch. Hannah shook her head and took his hand. Without a word, she led him to her bedroom.

He let her take the lead, and she began by taking off her boots. He yanked his boots off quickly. She pulled the sweatshirt and t-shirt over her head, leaving only a delicate blue cami to cover her soft, lightly golden skin and firm, perky breasts. He watched her every move, mesmerized.

Then she tugged on his sleeve. His shirt was next in line for removal. He'd never realized how many darn buttons were on that shirt until tonight. The unbuttoning must have progressed too slowly for Hannah because she took charge, and within seconds his shirt dropped to the floor.

She removed her jeans, so he removed his, taking care to quickly put his gun on the night table and return his attention to her almost naked body. He silently thanked the clouds for dimming the light of the moon at the exact moment his passion for her became apparent.

It had been years – almost five – since a woman had laid eyes on his unclothed body. But tonight, he would leave the past behind and focus his desires on Hannah and the here and now. They stood face to face. Hannah looked so sexy and yet angelic in her soft blue lingerie. Did she always dress so sweetly beneath her clothing?

They climbed warily into bed, watching each other, and he wondered if she was as nervous as he was. Once safely between the sheets, Trace took the lead. He pulled her close, so they lay like snuggling spoons. With a sigh, Oatie circled, then flopped down on the floor next to Hannah.

"I've never done this before," she whispered, her anxious body vibrating against his.

Seriously? Does she mean what I think she means?

Not wanting anything to ruin this moment, he kissed her neck and returned the whisper. "We're just going to sleep tonight if that's okay with you."

Her body relaxed, the trembling stopped. He felt her snuggle closer, warming his chest with her back. *She smells heavenly. This feels so right.*

HANNAH OPENED HER EYES. The sun peeked over the tops of the surrounding hills sending its rays through the window. The mattress sagged slightly, reminding her that she wasn't alone. For a few seconds, she lay perfectly still, enjoying the comforting sound of Trace's rhythmical breathing.

Eventually, she rolled over, gently, quietly. Her gaze softened, admiring him, marveling at his presence in her bed. *It's not a dream.* His cinnamon brown hair was slightly tousled, his long lashes resting like a baby's on his cheeks. The lips she loved to kiss were slightly parted, relaxed, and irresistible. When she leaned over and tenderly kissed them, his blue eyes opened.

"Mornin', sunshine."

She tilted her head toward the end of the bed.

"Ugh," he groaned, making her giggle. "No wonder I felt cramped all night. Oatie, get off the bed."

She pushed closer to Trace's warm body. "He likes it up here."

"Well, sure. So do I. But if all three of us are going to sleep together, we're going to need a bigger bed."

She liked the sound of that.

"Would you make some coffee while I take a quick shower?" she asked.

He'd propped himself up, leaning back on several pillows with his hands behind his head. An irresistible grin spread across his face, and she blushed when she realized he was studying her nearly naked body.

"Yes, ma'am. I can do that. Don't use up all the hot water, though. I'm getting in the shower right after you."

After a quick breakfast of coffee and farm-fresh, scrambled eggs, they fed the horses and the chickens.

Next, Hannah watched a saddling demonstration, and then Trace gave her a boost up onto Clark's back.

Trace wiggled his eyebrows, grinning up at her. "You do look mighty fine up there, ma'am." His fingers paused on her calf. "And you know what they say? If you climb onto the saddle, be ready for the ride."

She feigned prim consternation. "Hmm. Is that saying about horseback riding or something else, perhaps?"

"You are determined to keep me on my toes, aren't you?"

"Pretty much, yes."

Their banter continued as Trace gave her a few pointers about the use of the reins, the pressure of her knees and heels, and the tone of her voice. She gasped with apprehension as he took the reins in his hand and led Clark slowly around the corral, but she soon relaxed. "Not bad for a city girl," he said, after helping her dismount. "We'll head out after Rosa arrives with our picnic lunch."

A phone company truck pulled in just as riding lesson number one came to an end. Trace showed the repairman where the problem was, and Hannah asked if he needed access to the interior of the house. He didn't.

"What happened here?"

Trace was quick to reply. "We don't know. Phone quit

working sometime after 9:00 p.m. I discovered the damage a few hours later."

The small man peered closely at the wiring. "Looks like vandalism, Mr. McAllister."

Hannah's jaw dropped. "Vandalism? You mean someone deliberately destroyed the phone cable?" She shot Trace an accusatory glare. "You never mentioned that."

"Didn't want you to worry. It was late." He spoke as if this vandalism was no big deal. "Could have been a teenage prank."

"This far from town? I know you don't believe that."

"Maybe a beaver?" he said with a sheepish grin.

She didn't see the humor and folded her arms.

Trace nodded and decided his only way out was to come clean. "Lewissa did seem agitated last night, so it's a real possibility that someone was here. Someone with a knife sharp enough to skin a—"

"Pretty sure that someone had a decent pair of wire cutters," said the repairman. "And lookie here." He stuck his index finger into a hole in the dirt. It was a tight fit. "Any idea what might have made these holes? There's plenty of 'em."

Hannah knelt to get a closer look at the trail of holes. "Last night's vandal wore stilettos," she said matter-of-factly.

The two men stared at her, confused.

"English, please. You're talking to country boys."

"High heels. Ultra-thin high heels. You know, women's shoes?"

Trace's eyebrows drew in, but he looked doubtful. "Are you sure?"

"Pretty sure."

The repairman handed Trace the completed work order to sign, but Hannah intercepted the hand-off.

She signed it, handed it back, then looked up at Trace. She knew only one person around here who could manage stilettos in the dirt. *Callie*. The thought of that girl being here, sabotaging her phone, awakened a new determination in Hannah, especially now that Trace didn't seem to buy her stiletto story.

She tried to put herself in his shoes – his boots, rather. He'd known Callie ever since she was a little girl. Now was not the time to argue. She wanted their picnic to go without a hitch. But later, the gloves were coming off.

ELEVEN

Rosa and the repairman passed each other on the driveway. Their picnic lunch had arrived, and it was time to lock the doors and mount up.

Trace insisted that Hannah ride Clark, saying he was older, a hand shorter, and less spirited than Lewissa. His reasoning made sense, so she didn't object even though she was a little disappointed. She'd hoped to ride the mare.

Just as Trace had promised, they rode side-by-side, slow and easy. Oatie took the lead most of the time, veering off now and then to chase down a critter or investigate an interesting smell. As they ambled from one side of the vast pasture to the other, a red fox crossed their path. The horses were unconcerned. Hannah gazed at a pair of hawks soaring high above. Then laughed when several marmots poked their heads out from a small, rocky rise, creating a silly version of the carnival game Whack-a-Mole in her mind.

She noticed one of her favorite spots, slightly to the east. She'd walked there on several occasions intending to capture the serenity of the small oasis on paper. There, under a dozen shimmering aspens flowed a narrow creek that tumbled over and around a small outcropping of rocks.

"Can we spend a little time over there?" she asked.

"Sure. On our way back, if that's okay."

There was so much about this man that she adored. Everything was okay today.

They reached a long, metal gate, and Trace dismounted. He surprised her by handing over Lewissa's reins, and she regarded him with uncertainty.

"Once I get this gate open," he said, "I want you to take her with you and Clark to the other side. We're entering national forest land at this point."

She glanced at Lewissa. "Hear that? You're going to come with me."

Lewissa snorted, making both riders smile.

From then on, they rode single file on the narrow, uphill trail that headed northeast. The pleasant sound of the horses' plodding hooves was interrupted only when a squirrel objected to their presence.

In time, they reached a clearing, a high meadow covered with bold Indian Paint Brush and delicate Wild Blue Flax. Trace swung easily off Lewissa and went to Hannah's side, holding up his hands to help her down. It wasn't long before she realized his assistance was not only a gentlemanly gesture, but also a necessary one.

"Oh, my knees!" she groaned, grabbing his arms. "They're not working right."

"Yeah, that happens." He gave her an understanding smile. "I've been riding since before I could walk. Sometimes even my knees get stiff after a long day in the saddle."

He tossed the reins loosely over the saddles and let the horses wander off, exploring freely on their own. Hannah watched anxiously as Lewissa and Clark stepped closer and closer to the edge of a steep cliff.

"Isn't that dangerous?"

"For us two-footed mammals, maybe. For the horses? Nah. They think it's interesting."

Hannah wasn't too sure about that. She'd rather see them tied up to a tree, safe – and bored. She called to Lewissa, who turned and trotted right over to her.

"How did you do that?" Did he honestly want horse information from Hannah? That seemed odd.

"Do what?"

"Become the leader of this small herd?"

"I'm the leader?" she asked, brushing away a few flies from Lewissa's face as if she'd been around horses since childhood.

"It's looking that way. What have you been doing with these horses? Casting magic spells?"

Hannah laughed, wishing that were possible, then went on to describe her typical ranch day.

"First, I sit on the bench near the corral for a while. I talk to them, I feed them, but mostly I'm just there, silent with them."

Trace looked impressed. "Well, horse experts do say that hanging out with a horse does the most for bonding. You're living proof of that."

They walked the clearing, stretching their legs and holding hands, enjoying the views and the serenity of the moment.

"What else do you do besides bond with the horses?"

He wants to know more about me. I like that.

"When I'm not with you, I've been busy cleaning and making plans for the house. Back in Phoenix, I sang karaoke on the weekends, and I loved to dance. I still sing and dance here at my ranch. I'm pretty good – as long as no one is looking or listening."

His smile, broader and more engaging than ever

before, warmed her heart. She'd save explaining about her unique air guitar abilities for another day, or maybe, she'd put that one behind her. After spending a week in her new environment, that activity seemed a touch too wacky.

They drank some water from Trace's canteen, then rounded up the horses. By the time they arrived at Hannah's favorite, shady spot, they'd worked up hearty appetites.

Trace spread the blanket, and Hannah, with outspread arms, inhaled deeply. "Smells almost like fresh cut lumber out here. I've always loved that smell."

Hunger replaced her brief olfactory distraction, and she unpacked Rosa's delicious-looking picnic lunch. Oatie observed her every move, sniffing the air with appreciation and anticipation. The horses grazed calmly nearby.

They settled in across from each other, too busy eating to speak at first. Hannah munched on cut-up fruits and vegetables, pieces of cheese and slices of homemade sourdough bread, but completely avoided the beef jerky. Fortunately, the sight of the stiff, dried meat didn't turn her stomach like a hunk of animal flesh on a plate would have.

"The potato salad is out of this world," she murmured, her mouth full.

"So is the view," he said, looking into her eyes, making her blush. "This is your favorite spot, huh?"

She nodded and admitted that every time she'd been here, she felt at peace.

"How many times have you been here?"

"As you know, I haven't lived here very long, but I've communed with these aspen trees three times already."

The meal ended beautifully, with two glasses of champagne and some tiny, bite-sized strawberry tarts. Lulled into a post-meal bliss, Hannah rested her head on Trace's shoulder, hoping to remember this peaceful outing forever.

Without warning, the weather changed. Trace, believing the cloud build-up, the wind gusts, and the drop in temperature would soon pass, suggested they wait it out. Hannah, thrilled to curl up in a blanket with him beside the bubbling brook and beneath her favorite trees, relaxed in his arms.

I cannot imagine a better afternoon than this, not even in a dream.

The tree trunks creaked in protest as the intense wind picked up even more, causing the leaves to rustle loudly as it pushed through. Hannah, no longer feeling peaceful, had just begun to voice a suggestion when several loud *cracks* silenced her.

The trees towering above them shook violently, and both horses squealed, rearing up with alarm. Oatie yelped, and Trace grabbed Hannah, rolling them roughly away from the bending trees. The dream had become a nightmare, playing out at lightning speed. Trace pulled her to her feet, and they stared in horror as three of the aspens crashlanded where they had been lying just seconds before.

Even Trace seemed troubled. He kept shaking his head. "I've never seen anything like that. I'm sorry, Hannah. That was a close one." He scrutinized the area, looking unsettled. "Mother Nature at work, I guess. And being in the wrong place at the wrong time."

"Have you angered her lately?" she teased, hoping to lessen the tension. "Maybe forgot flowers on her birthday?"

"Whose birthday?"

"Mother Nature's."

He smiled at her sweet joke, then pulled her closer to him. "That's enough adventure for today, I reckon."

Trace rounded up the horses, which were instinctively keeping their distance from the trees. Hannah dashed back for the blanket and found something else.

"Trace! Come take a look."

He knelt beside her. "When we first arrived here today, I noticed a scent like the lumber section at Home

Depot. Remember? Look at this." She sprinkled tiny tan particles into his hand.

"Sawdust?" His jaw dropped as he examined the trees. "A beaver would have made neater cuts," Trace mused, curious. "He also would have finished the job." He jabbed a finger at the wood, shaking his head. "I can't believe it. Those are saw marks! These trees were *tampered* with!"

That made no sense. "Who would want to harm a tree? What's the point in that?"

Trace didn't speak and appeared deep in thought as he helped her mount up.

Within fifteen minutes, they were back among clucking chickens and mooing cows

"Hannah, I need to run back to my place," he said reluctantly. "I'll be gone a couple of hours. Do me a favor. Stay inside and keep your doors locked the rest of the day, okay?"

"Sure. When you get back, can you stay for dinner?"

He faked an expression of intense thought. "Tell you what. I'll not only stay for dinner, I'll stick around for dessert." With a charming wink, he turned toward his truck, then glanced back at Hannah. "Do you have a gun?"

"Why would I have a gun?"

"Oh, I don't know. For protection from creepy, phony,

satellite dish installers? Stuff like that. Have you ever shot one?"

"A creepy satellite dish installer?" She giggled until she saw the serious look on Trace's face. She gave his question some thought and came up with a real answer. "Yeah, a couple of times, but that was years ago. Not sure I know how anymore."

He leaned closer and kissed her cheek. "That's going to change real soon."

TWELVE

In her wildest dreams, Hannah never thought she'd *need* a gun. That reality was frightening and difficult to grasp. So she switched topics from guns to the coming evening's meal. She stared helplessly into the pantry, frustrated by the miserable selection of meal-making ingredients. *Maybe I should have waited a little longer before inviting him to dinner.*

On her first shopping trip, the idea of preparing a special meal for company had been the furthest thing from her mind, so she was unprepared. After finding tomato sauce, onions, Parmesan cheese, and tofu, she concluded that spaghetti was a possibility. She'd add a splash of red wine to the sauce; the rest of the bottle would end up in their drinking glasses.

She frowned. *Note to self: Purchase some wine glasses.*

What else? Sautéed zucchini would go well with the spaghetti, but what could she serve for dessert? Trace had mentioned dessert. She knew he'd been teasing, but she wanted to serve something, and her options were sadly limited. Individually wrapped squares of ultra-dark chocolate would have to do, though they were a far cry from the homemade fruit tarts Trace was accustomed to.

Another note to self: Purchase a cookbook.

The phone rang, jarring her from her thoughts. She smiled and picked up. It must be Trace. Who else knew her number?

"Hello?"

No response.

"Hello? Hello? Trace, is that you? I can't hear you!" Were there still problems with her phone line? "Hello? Anyone there?"

She set the phone down, annoyed, and resumed her preparations. With the spaghetti sauce simmering, the zucchini cut up and ready for sautéing, she set the kitchen island. Tonight, they would pretend it was a table. She added one final touch, a candle she'd found when she'd first searched through the cabinets. After lighting it and standing back to admire her work, a distant memory came to mind in the form of a vision. One of her mother lighting a candle while saying, *Everything looks good by candlelight.* Her sweet reverie came to a sudden end when the phone rang again.

"Hello? Can you hear me?"

Still, nothing.

"If you're trying to scare me into becoming a gun owner, this is not the way to do it." Did she hear breathing on the other end of the line? No, that only happens in horror movies. "This isn't funny. Stop it."

She'd call Trace and sort this out, but just as she was about to dial, the phone rang again. After the third call from no one, she'd had enough. Either the phone still had technical difficulties, Trace was playing games, or...? She didn't want to think about other possibilities.

Quickly, she made the call.

"Hello, McAllister Ranch. Rosa speaking."

"Hi, Rosa. It's Hannah. How are you?"

"Just fine, hon. How about yourself?"

"I'm fine too, but I'm having trouble with incoming calls on my phone, so I thought I'd try calling out. I can hear you just fine, and you hear me too, right?"

"Sure do. Loud and clear." Rosa's tone was as upbeat and friendly as ever.

"I think Trace has been calling me, but each time, no sound came through."

"There is no way it could have been him."

Goosebumps tickled all over her body. "Why not?"

"He's been at the small bunkhouse for over an hour with Callie. Said they needed to talk. There's no phone in there. And his ranch phone is sitting right with me."

"Oh, okay." She thanked Rosa and hung up. She wasn't sure what bothered her more, the possibility that a creepy, phone-calling prankster might exist, or the fact that Trace was in the bunkhouse with Callie.

TRACE GRABBED a wooden chair from the table, turned it around, and sat resting his arms on its back. Callie stood a few feet away looking down her nose at him, her arms crossed under her breasts making them perkier than they need be.

The lighting in the bunkhouse was complimentary, casting a silhouetted shadow of the slender, but well-endowed young gal. She wore a tight pair of cut-off jean shorts and a white crop top, obviously flaunting her wares and hoping to get his attention. And oh, she had his attention all right. For the first time, he noticed, *really* noticed, that the teen's body had become a woman's body – a magnificent one. When had that happened?

Tonight, she'd turned up the heat with her sexuality and her attempts to seduce him. What she didn't understand was that he wasn't going to fall for her antics. Not now, not ever. But that wasn't what he'd come here to talk about.

He wanted answers to his questions about the damaged phone cable and the suspicious holes in the ground. Hannah had said that high-heeled women's shoes had made them. That description fit the ones Callie had worn in his den the night of the vandalism.

"What were you doing at Hannah's place last night? You've got no business there."

She rolled her eyes, then scowled at him as if he was crazy. "I haven't been over there since the day you made me do some shopping for that stupid, city slicker bitch."

He stood up, furious, and threw the chair across the room. "You're out of line, Callie. Way out of line."

Shocked, she cowered in the corner, acting as if she'd come face to face with Jack the Ripper.

He shook his head even more disgusted. "Stop with the drama. You know I would never lay a hand on you or any other woman for that matter. But you, young lady, had better start telling the truth because I'm running out of patience. Admit it, you were at Hannah's place. Someone wearing high-heeled shoes was there, and you're the only one I know who has shoes like that."

"Well, it wasn't me, and you can't prove it was. Besides, what kind of fool would go walking around in the dirt in shoes like that?" She shook her head, her defiance giving way to more flirtation. "Definitely, not a country girl like me."

To Trace's disappointment, Callie confessed to nothing. She even assured him that she would never, ever do anything that would displease him. He cursed himself for failing to bring his cell phone. He could have used its camera to snap a photo of Callie's three pair of shoes. They were all lined up neatly against the wall by her bunk, and incriminating dirt still clung to the pair with the high heels. A mental picture would have to do for now.

TRACE HAD ASSURED her that he'd return in a couple of hours. Three and a half infuriating hours had now passed with no sign of him. Hannah glared at the simmering spaghetti sauce and contemplated tossing the whole thing down the drain.

She didn't need to be fawning over or cooking for a guy she'd only known a week, especially one who, apparently, wanted to spend time with a *sexy girl who knows cows*. In her mind, Callie *was* a cow. Her mom had been right when she'd warned her about men. *They will hurt you, then walk away, leaving you with all the trouble they created.*

Standing at the sink with her saucepan in hand, she heard a vehicle coming down the driveway. Oatie barked and wagged his tail, dashing to the door. Hannah recognized the sound of Trace's boots thumping slowly and steadily up the steps.

When she opened the door, his blue eyes sparkled, and he smiled warmly as if nothing was wrong. In his hands he held a small tray covered with foil. This cowboy looked every bit as good as any hot guy on the cover of a western romance novel. *Ugh! Not now. Be still, my heart.* For a moment, she let her protective guard down.

"Sorry, I'm late. I've brought a peace offering that we can cook tonight or save for another time."

Determined, she regained her train of thought. "I know why you're late. You were with Callie again." Her quivering voice betrayed her.

"Yes, I was. Want to know why?"

"No, I do not! The fact that you would leave my place and drive all the way back to her, then return late – well, that's all I need to know."

Knowing she'd melt at the mere sight of him, she averted her eyes and busied herself by carrying his *peace offering* to the kitchen counter. When she lifted the foil to peek at its contents, she froze with horror. Two hunks of reddish flesh, still oozing blood, lay there motionless, and unquestionably dead. Thoughts of

Buttercup sprang to her mind and she bolted toward the bathroom.

Trace followed and knocked tentatively at the partially open door. "What's the matter? Do you want my help?"

Severe nausea had triggered hyperventilation, which added dizziness to her distress. Sweat streamed down her face and dripped into the sink. Her condition deteriorated; she needed more than the sink. "Go away!" she managed to squeak. She didn't want him to see her kneeling at the toilet poised to vomit. Add a little anger and fury – it was not a pretty sight.

By the time she returned to the kitchen, he'd packed up the freshly butchered steaks, put them in the freezer, and washed all remnants of the uncooked meat from the tray.

"Better now?" His eyes were large and hopeful, like a puppy looking for approval.

"Yes, but why would you do that?" Her voice trembled. "You know I'm a vegetarian. The sight of raw meat makes me ill."

"I didn't know. I don't think the topic ever came up before tonight."

She thought about that. Hadn't she told him? Could he be right? Maybe. She made an effort to soften her voice a little. "Well, you know now."

"Do you eat any meat at all?"

"Eggs, once in a while, but if an animal has to be killed, I won't eat it."

He frowned, thinking hard about what she'd said. "So, now you're mad at me about the *meat?*" he asked, sounding slightly exasperated. "You do know I'm a cattle rancher? Do we need to add that to our lengthening list of personal problems?"

Hannah knew she shouldn't be angry about the steaks. Most people would love to receive such a gift. Somehow, they'd work out their cattle rancher vs. vegetarian issues, but Callie was still a problem. A serious problem.

He sighed. "Come and sit with me on the couch. Let me tell you about my conversation with Callie and the reason it took place." When he offered her his hand, she took it though her eyes looked down.

Oatie followed them to the loveseat and sat at their feet, listening to Trace's words. Whenever Trace paused, the dog glanced at Hannah, checking her reaction. His dark dog eyes seemed concerned.

"Let's see if I've got this right," Hannah said. "Finally, you think Callie came to my place – wearing her stilettos – and cut my phone line?"

"Yes, I'm almost positive."

"I do agree with your *who,* and we know the *what* and the *where,* but I don't understand the *why,*" she said, carefully studying his face and wondering if he had an answer.

He looked directly into her eyes. "Why? You said she's been trying to get you to leave from the day you two met. Isn't that enough?"

"I suppose so. She wants you, Trace. She thinks that I'm the only thing standing in her way."

He reached for her hand, and she gave it to him. "I also wonder if Callie had anything to do with cutting through the aspen trees."

"Really? That seems a little far-fetched. How would she even know that I liked to spend time there?"

"Exactly. How would she know? That's a damn good question. Maybe she's not involved in that. What I do know is that we can't credit Mother Nature for the deliberate cuts in those tree trunks. Someone, a human with a saw, made them."

Hannah slumped and then sighed. It seemed they couldn't get through a day without something strange and disconcerting obstructing their forward motion.

They moved to the larger sofa, along with Oatie, and lay down, wrapped in each other's arms. Through the window, they watched the sun disappear below the tree line, turning the sky into a rainbow of orange and indigo, and creating a perfect backdrop for the black silhouettes of swooping swallows.

"I'm hungry," he whispered into her ear. "Do you feel up to eating?"

"Maybe, but only a little." Reluctantly, she struggled upright, already missing his warmth. "I just need to boil water for the pasta and sauté the zucchini. Everything should be ready to eat in about twenty minutes."

"Sounds perfect. I left something in the truck, but I'll be right back. Come on, Oatie."

Hannah set the bottle of wine between the two place settings and lit the candle. By the time Trace and his dog returned, she was draining the water from the pasta.

"What took you so long? I was about to send out a search party."

He flinched slightly at her simple comment, and she didn't understand why. An itch perhaps?

"I checked the house's perimeter. We can't be too careful anymore, you know?"

Hannah spotted the bottle of champagne in his hand just as he eyed the red wine already set on their temporary table.

"I don't drink wine," he said gently, touching her cheek. "Only champagne, and just a little. But you can. You can have some of each."

Today's final note to self: Purchase fluted champagne glasses as well as Post-its for keeping track of information.

"Champagne is your drink of choice. Hmm, I think I knew that. Rosa said something about it the other night," she said, looking up into his eyes. "Trace, I sure hope the saying *opposites attract* is true. Almost every time we're together another difference or conflict arises. You only drink champagne, and I don't eat meat. Can we make this work?"

Trace smiled warmly, the twinkle back in his eyes. "Of course we can. Sometimes getting to know each other has its tumbles."

They managed to make it through the dinner hour without a hitch, their friendly conversation kept within the safe bounds of weather, Oatie, and Lewissa. The only time they approached a tension-fused topic was when Trace asked, "If you don't eat or cook meat, what am I chewing that *feels* like, you know, meat?"

A look of shock – or was that a grimace – appeared on his face when she informed him that he was eating tofu, but he wisely said nothing, though he seemed to have trouble swallowing.

THIRTEEN

Hannah stifled the laugh that threatened to escape her lips. The look on his face when she'd informed him that he'd just bitten into tofu was priceless. "Ready for dessert?" she asked.

"I'm always ready for dessert."

Hannah was referring to the dark chocolate, but she knew perfectly well he was thinking of something else. Regardless, he got chocolate. He ate it slowly, savoring its flavor. "Mm, mm. This is the best chocolate square I've ever eaten." He had a talent for teasing. Was that a cowboy thing?

He helped her place the dishes in the sink and then guided her toward the bedroom, struggling to undo the many buttons on his shirt as they walked. "There is something you should know," he said, his serious tone betrayed by the twinkle in his eye. "I have a rule."

Trace was in a playful mood tonight. *Well, two could play the game*. She shrugged and feigned a look of boredom. "So? Everybody's got a few rules. You've only got one?"

His look of deep thinking increased her curiosity. "Yes, for tonight, only one. I must know a woman at least two weeks before I go to bed with her. Good rule, huh?"

The charming grin was back. Hannah blinked, unsure of how she felt about his rule, and shoved his bare chest away from her. Was he teasing? Hadn't he already been to bed with her?

"And just how many women have you known for at least two weeks?"

"Nope. I'm not going there, but since you're still a—" He hesitated, then smiled again. "Well, you know. I think we should wait even longer. Don't you?"

An odd mixture of relief and frustration bubbled through her as they undressed for what she assumed would be a good night's sleep. She joined him under the covers, happy to snuggle up with him. She loved his scent, the feel of his skin, and the way this big, tough cowboy caressed her with such tenderness. Just being near him raised her body heat to a degree she'd never thought possible.

Trace lifted his head, supporting it with his arm, and she rolled toward him. He watched her intently, as if she was a subject to be studied, then reached over and tickled her bottom lip with his finger.

"I noticed the pictures sitting on the mantel," he said. "Tell me about them."

"Did you recognize the drawing of Lewissa?"

"I did think it looked like her, but some horses look alike. You drew that?"

She nodded. "Drawing is my favorite hobby, and one I've been sadly neglecting lately."

"Amazing! I had no idea you were an artist. You turned plain white paper into an equestrian masterpiece complete with texture and emotion."

Slightly surprised, Hannah beamed with pride. "And I had no idea you were such an articulate art critic."

"I know talent when I see it," he whispered, weaving his fingers through her hair.

He just keeps getting better and better!

"The woman with me in one of the photos is my mom, Lillian, at my high school graduation. And the other photo was taken when Rick and I were in a dance contest." She frowned, seeing a flicker of doubt cross his eyes. "Does it bother you that I have his picture displayed there?"

"No. Rick was your friend, and I get that. It's just

that…" He took a deep breath and let it out. "He looks vaguely familiar, though I doubt we ever met. Hmm."

"It's common knowledge that everyone has a doppelganger somewhere on the planet. You've probably seen that person at some point during your lifetime, that's all."

"A what?" Trace said with a frown. "In my entire life, I've never said that word or heard anyone else use it. Did you just make that up?"

"No, no! That's a real word," she giggled. "It means lookalike."

"Oh, okay. Then, yeah, I guess it's possible."

Enough talk for now. She began nibbling his neck instead. With a manly moan, he returned her sweet gesture.

Suddenly, Oatie emitted a deep, vibrating growl. Hannah's eyes sprang open, her heart racing.

Trace was already up and pulling on his jeans. "It's probably just the wind."

"Really? Does he usually growl at the wind? He didn't when he slept here the other night, and it was pretty windy then."

"No, he doesn't, but the moon is almost full. His senses could be on extra high alert." He tugged on his boots. "I won't be able to sleep until I know we're all good."

He produced a handgun from under his pillow, then instructed Hannah and Oatie to stay put.

Neither obeyed. Instead, they followed quietly behind him.

"Do you have a flashlight?" he whispered.

"You'll find two in the drawer to the right of the sink. Why are we whispering?"

He didn't reply but put a finger to his lips.

Oatie growled again, making a soft, throaty sound as he crept toward the sliding glass door on the north side of the kitchen. Once there, he barked furiously, his snarling lips curled back, exposing his teeth. The adorable cattle dog had transformed into a wolf ready to attack, and the sight frightened Hannah.

"I've never seen him like this. Are you sure he's all right?"

Trace's jaw looked tight. "He's just doing his job. Oatie doesn't growl at deer or elk, but he might act this way if a pack of coyotes or a bear was close to the house."

He flipped on the outside lights, his gun ready. "Don't worry. Whatever upset the dog now knows we're aware of its presence. It's likely already gone. Why don't you go back to bed? I want to check all the doors, make sure they're closed tight and locked."

"All right," she replied, uneasy. "But I won't be able

to sleep. I feel like I've had a dozen cups of strong coffee."

"Got any tea?"

She smiled. "I do. Some chamomile." She tiptoed to the sink and filled a kettle with water.

"Let me do that. Go on back to bed. This won't take long. Water boils quickly at this altitude."

She went, relieved when Oatie followed and jumped onto the bed. She heard the sound of cupboards opening and closing as he searched for the tea. Minutes later, he returned with a cup of hot tea in one hand and two small objects in the other.

"Are these yours?" he asked.

"No. Where did you find them?"

He handed her the tea. "One was on the top shelf of the cupboard above the stove. The other was inside the ceiling light."

"You looked inside the ceiling light for tea?" She chuckled. "Never mind, I withdraw the question."

He wasn't laughing. "Hannah, these are bugging devices. Someone has bugged the place. I'm calling the sheriff in the morning."

"WHO TURNED ON THE HIGH BEAMS?" Trace's sleep-filled voice croaked as sunshine streamed in from the window and onto his face.

"Uh, I think that was probably your old friend, Mother Nature," Hannah replied, still drowsy. She put her lips close to Trace's ear. "Blinded by the light..." she sang.

Trace kept his eyes closed. "You're smiling, aren't you? I can hear it in your voice. How can you be so playful this morning? I know you didn't sleep much more than I did."

They'd both overslept and would've happily lounged in bed a bit longer had it not been for Oatie. Judging by his energy and persistence, he needed to go out.

"Okay, okay," Trace grumbled, rolling out of bed. "Hold your horses. I'm coming."

He pulled on his jeans but didn't bother zipping them. Nor did he bother with a shirt. Oatie stuck to his heels. Opening the door, he did a double-take, surprised by what he saw. He'd come face to face with Jane Carter, the sheriff. Her arm was raised as if she were about to knock.

She smirked, scrutinizing his lack of clothing. "Huh, I can almost see why Callie has the hots for you."

"That is *not* amusing," he said, leaning against the doorway as Oatie bounded past him.

"Oh, I thought it was."

What was she doing here? He'd planned to call her about the bugs he'd found, but he hadn't had a chance yet. A sudden thought came to mind. Could she possibly have been the one to plant the bugs in the first place? No, that would be borderline crazy, not to mention illegal. Then again, crazy was rapidly becoming the word of the week.

Jane shrugged, and just like that, she was all business. "I stopped by to talk with Hannah. Can I come in?"

"Sure," said Hannah, already by Trace's side, a bit tousled and obviously curious. "How did you get here so fast, Sheriff?"

"You were expecting me?"

Trace jumped in. "I had planned on calling you this morning, but we just woke up. Had a strange night. You first, though. I'll make some coffee while you tell us what brings you way out here today."

Jane nodded. "The truth is," she said, leaning against the island countertop, "I've never been convinced that Rick's death was an accident. Had a gut feeling about it right from the start."

"We had the same—"

Trace cut Hannah off. "We talked about all the possibilities, tried to make sense of the whole thing, but came up empty."

"Huh. Well, I did some snooping around, called in a

few favors. Got no real answers, mind you, but more information than we had before." She took a sip of coffee, then turned and stared directly at Hannah. "You may already know what I am about to say, so feel free to stop me if this is old news."

Jane's discovery? Rick had a twin brother named Rudy. They were born near Pomona, California. Somewhere between the ages of three and five, they were placed separately with foster parents. "Their whereabouts was sketchy after that," Jane explained. "The paperwork might have been lost in the huge California system."

"Were they identical twins?" Trace asked.

"I don't know. Maybe. Maybe not." Turning toward Hannah, her eyes narrowed skeptically. "I find it strange that you did not know your best friend – the man you chose to share the ranch with after leaving Phoenix – had a brother."

Hannah straightened, looking offended. "No, I am positive he never mentioned having a brother. In fact, he claimed to have no family at all."

Jane tapped her fingers on the counter. "I suppose in his mind that might have been true. No one seems to know what happened to the twin's birth mother and father, and foster homes don't always work out. Rick might have blocked his past from his thinking, and Rudy could be deceased by now." Jane emptied her coffee cup and edged toward the door. "So none of this rings a bell? Jars your thinking? Inspires more questions or, better yet, a few answers?"

Both Trace and Hannah shook their heads, and Jane turned back to leave. Her inquisitive eyes landed on the two small bugs lying on the shelf by the door. Putting gloves on, she picked them up.

"Either of you want to tell me about these? Most folks don't bug their own homes, you know. I've got a handful of these short-range bugs back at the station in my desk. I rarely use them, though. From a technical aspect, they're not much good."

When Trace shrugged, Hannah did the same. He was relieved she'd taken his cue to keep quiet.

"I found them last night when I was looking for tea," he told Jane. "That's why we were going to call you this morning."

With a nod, Jane removed a Ziploc bag from her back pocket and dropped in the bugs. "I'd better take a look around."

Trace explained where he'd found the devices, and Jane headed to the opposite end of the house to conduct her own search. Returning, she said she'd found nothing.

"I'll get back to you about these," she said, holding up the bag containing the two bugs.

"Who has access to your office?" Trace asked.

The sheriff turned and walked briskly out the door to her patrol car as if the question had never been asked. Had she not heard him? He wanted to ask again, but the car was already pulling away.

While Oatie nosed around the yard, Trace stood on the porch thinking of the possibilities, all of them strange and getting stranger by the minute. When he went back inside, Hannah stared at him with a look he couldn't read.

"What? What's the matter?" he asked.

She hesitated, suddenly shy. "It's just that I'm not used to seeing you quite like this."

"Like what?" He glanced down, remembering his bare feet, his bare chest, and the unzipped jeans that would have slipped down had they not fit so snugly over his hips. He chuckled. "I was in a hurry. Hang on. I'll be right back."

FOURTEEN

Trace returned quickly, dressed and ready to greet the world. He found Hannah waiting for him on the back porch with two steaming cups of coffee. The morning sun warmed their faces and soothed their minds, at least for the moment.

Hannah took a sip of her coffee. "Do you think she knows more than she's saying?"

He didn't want to worry her; nevertheless, he shared one of his thoughts. "I'm certain Jane knows more than she's telling us, but she didn't come to share information. She was here on a fact-finding mission. I'm afraid we sorely disappointed her."

"How come you gave me the evil eye and cut me off each time I began to speak?"

He had a method to his madness. "One word," he told

her. "Callie. She's an immature kid who is known for making bad choices. And she's the sheriff's daughter."

The shocked look on Hannah's face alerted him to the fact that she'd been unaware of that relationship. "Kid? She's only a few years younger than me."

"That may be, but you seem a lot older." He caught her injured grimace just in time. "In a good way!" he added, hoping to repair the sudden damage.

"No. There's no good way for a woman to seem a lot older."

He scratched his head, embarrassed. "Yeah, that didn't come out right. I meant wiser, more adult-like. But since the subject of age has come up, how old do you think I am?"

"Does it matter?" She tilted her head. So did the dog.

"Not to me, but it might to you."

Now, with a mischievous glint in her eyes, she studied him up and down, smiling all the while. "I think you are older than me and younger than my mom."

"That was safe but far too vague to be considered a real answer. How old is your mom?"

By the look on her face and the hands on her hips, he could tell she wasn't falling for his tactic.

"No way! She would not be happy if I told you her age or any other personal detail. She's always been a very private woman."

Hannah's comment rendered him speechless for a second, but then he found a clever way to change tactics.

"You won't tell me your mom's age. I get that. How about your dad? Men don't care if their ages are known."

She bit her lip and glanced to the side. "I have no dad."

"That, my dear, is biologically impossible."

Her scowl was determined. "Well, that's my answer."

"Okay," Trace replied, somewhat annoyed that he'd gotten nowhere with his line of questioning. He decided to show her what sharing was all about. "Well, FYI, I will turn thirty-one in a few months. I thought I was in love once, but I was wrong about that. And I've never been married. There, that's my story. Maybe someday you will tell me yours. More coffee?"

Hannah still wasn't forthcoming; instead, she went back to their earlier discussion. "Why didn't you tell the sheriff about Callie? Yes, Jane's her mother, but she's also the law around here."

He'd given this some thought and had a disquieting hunch that Callie engaged in something far more nefarious than expediting Hannah's departure.

"I don't want Jane to say anything in front of Callie that might tip her off to our suspicions. I hate to say it, but Callie might be the key to everything. Right now, the accident is Jane's only concern. I'd like to keep it that way for a while."

"So we're conducting our own investigation like Sherlock and Dr. Watson? Or Walt Longmire and Vic Moretti?"

"Yep. And we're going to get serious about that task."

"Okay. Let's get organized." She pulled out paper and a pen, and they began to construct three lists: Known Facts, Odd Occurrences, and Loose Assumptions.

KNOWN FACTS

A dead body was found in the Range Rover (positive ID pending).

Rick had a twin brother (identical twin?) whose existence/whereabouts is unknown.

Rick – or a man who looks like Rick – emptied the bank account in Phoenix.

One of Trace's cows died from poison found in the stock tank.

Aspen trees were tampered with where Hannah often sat.

Hannah's phone cable was cut.

An imposter satellite dish installer had been snooping inside the house.

Electronic listening devices were found.

Odd Occurrences

The horses and the dog had several episodes of extreme agitation.

Loose Assumptions

Rick might be alive.

Rick could be dead. (If so, who killed him?)

If Rick is alive, an unknown person is dead.

Callie wants Hannah gone. (* Hannah thinks this should be a Known Fact.)

Callie wants Trace all to herself. (* Ditto!)

"SO, NOW WHAT?"

Trace thought for a moment. "For starters, let's see if we can connect some of these dots."

She sat up straight. "I just remembered that while I was waiting for you to come back last night, I received three phone calls."

"Well, aren't you popular?"

"No, it wasn't like that. Every time I answered the phone, no one spoke. I'm sure someone was on the line because I heard, you know, breathing."

Trace gave her new information some thought. "It could have been a prank caller, or someone reaching the wrong number but too embarrassed to admit their mistake, or—" He looked her in the eye, reluctant to share his honest opinion. "Or the caller intended to intimidate you."

She nodded soberly. "That's what it felt like."

By the time their first brainstorming session concluded, they were both mentally fatigued and still feeling the effects from the previous, sleepless night. They needed to relax, to get away from all the weirdness. Trace knew just the place.

"Didn't you tell me that one of the reasons you agreed to live on a ranch with Rick was that you wanted to participate in some outdoor adventure?" he asked, wisely moving from the topic of intimidation.

"Yes. And work on my drawing, and maybe learn more about growing herbs that I could use to make essential oils."

He grinned. "Well, I can help you with the outdoor adventure part. Pack a bag with the warmest clothes you have; layers will work best. The adventure begins in about thirty minutes."

Leaving her to pack, Trace checked on and fed all the animals, then called Rosa.

TRACE KEPT HER IN SUSPENSE, stating only that their first stop was at his ranch. She assumed his promised adventure included a sleepover due to the amount of feed he'd given the horses and the chickens.

Rosa looked excited when she greeted them from the veranda. It seemed all the women in Trace's life enjoyed pleasing him, Hannah noted wryly.

"Everything is ready to go, Mr. McAllister."

"All right, then. I'll get the Ranger."

Hannah turned toward Rosa. "What in the world is Trace up to? A ranger is coming with us?"

Rosa chuckled, then invited her inside. "No, dear. Mr. McAllister is taking you to his secret, private ranch. I'm sure he will tell you the whole story someday. All I can say is that you are the first woman he has ever taken up there."

Hannah lifted one eyebrow. "You've never been there?"

"Oh, well," Rosa said, slightly flustered. "I don't count. Even so, I haven't been up there since his father's —" She stopped, hand over her mouth. "Oh, my, I've said too much."

Hannah was confused. "On the contrary, you haven't even told me about the ranger."

"Ah," she smiled. "The Ranger is the off-road vehicle you'll be riding in."

Right on cue, they heard the roar of the arriving transportation. Rosa gave Hannah a hug, then they picked up several bags filled with food items and walked back outside.

Rosa placed the bags in the cooler, smiling and humming all the while.

"Hop in and buckle up," Trace said, grinning. Oatie had already found a cozy spot between the cooler and several duffle bags. Hannah climbed in, then watched and listened as Trace and Rosa exchange a few last words.

"We'll be back tomorrow before noon."

"All right, Mr. McAllister." Looking directly at Trace, she frowned, seeming concerned. "You're sure about this?"

"I'm sure. It's time. Giving Hannah a safe, stress-free day and an adventure is just the motivation I've needed all these years. Plus, I like her. A lot."

"I know, and…"

Their quiet words faded into the breeze, leaving Hannah curious. She leaned back in her seat and breathed deeply, letting go of all her worries and glowing with anticipation. With Trace at the wheel, they rolled back onto the dirt road, made a left turn, and headed north. Hannah had never been farther than the long driveway that led into his ranch. Now, up ahead, she faced new scenery, new experiences. She was ready for the day, the adventure, and she tingled at the thought of another night sleeping snuggled up to Trace.

The Ranger's engine roared as they bounced and bumped over the neglected, boulder-filled trail. They stopped only twice along the way. The first time occurred after they'd driven for about an hour. Trace needed to cut away a fallen tree that blocked the path. While the chainsaw buzzed, the dog jumped out to stretch his legs, and Hannah took the opportunity to observe a handsome, rugged man at work. On the second stop, they simply opened, then closed a gate.

Are we there yet?" she asked. She felt certain their destination had history – any *secret ranch* would – but Trace remained silent, merely pointing out the 360-degree view. That's when she saw the lake. It was the most breathtaking sight she'd ever laid eyes on.

Trace slowed to a crawl. Oatie jumped out of the back and bounded off, seeming to know right where he was going. The dog navigated the terrain with far more grace than the vehicle, which rocked, tipped, and got stuck several times. Hannah, grateful for the firm grip of her seatbelt, began to wonder what she'd gotten herself into. Finally, the Ranger came to a full stop, and Trace pulled on the brake.

With the engine off, the sudden silence tickled her ears while her body still vibrated from the rough ride. She stepped carefully from the vehicle, then gasped in amazement when she spotted it. A rustic cabin tucked away in the midst of a rare grove of low-growing pines, dwarfed by the altitude and severe weather – a fact Trace had recently shared. Too awestruck to giggle, she thought to herself, *This isn't Kansas anymore.* She'd entered a whole different and distant world.

"Where are we?" she whispered, not wanting to disturb the tranquility.

"This is the first piece of land west of the Mississippi that my family ever owned," said Trace with pride, his voice was slightly hoarse with emotion. "My great-great-grandfather, Mack McAllister, homesteaded this 40-acre section. He stumbled upon it and fell in love with the lake and the land." He shrugged. "The ground's no good for ranching, but, even though it was an impractical decision, it was a start."

They walked hand in hand toward the pristine lake, twenty yards away, and stood at its bank. The water was shiny and smooth, like a mirror, and as still as the air around it. A pair of red-tailed hawks circled above, calling out to each other, and the dog's curious eyes followed their high altitude dance.

"Tell me more."

Trace let out a long breath. "Not much to tell. Dad used to bring me up here to fish and talk about cows.

Generations ago, that first small herd of cattle didn't do well. The altitude was too high, and grass wouldn't grow, but great-great-grandfather didn't know about things like that. He came from a family of statesmen, not ranchers. This place has been called the *No Cow Ranch* ever since." He chuckled and squeezed her hand. "Cows or no cows, this was a special place for my dad."

A memory must have surfaced, transforming his expression, and he continued. "One day, about fifteen years ago, Mother and Father had a huge argument, which was unusual for them. They weren't good at fighting with each other. Anyway, my dad stormed out and rode away on his favorite horse, Rowdy."

"And he came all the way up here? On horseback?"

Trace gave a subtle nod.

"Did he come alone?"

"Nope." Trace's sad eyes stared out over the water, his expression resigned. "He brought an unopened bottle of Wild Turkey with him. When he didn't come home, Mother, Rosa, and I went searching for him. Troy, my older brother, helped too."

"I take it you found him up here?"

Another nod. "He'd had an accident. We had to put the horse out of its misery and dad in a wheelchair. He's been paralyzed from the waist down ever since that night."

Her heart broke for him. "I'm so sorry. Are you sure you want to be here with me?"

"Yes." He turned toward her and held her gaze. "I care for you, Hannah, and I want you to know me better before we take our relationship too much further." He smiled gently. "And to be honest, I also wanted to get you away from the Lucky 7."

"The Lucky 7?"

"Yes. I reside at The McAllister Ranch, we call it The Big Mack for short, and you're at the Lucky 7."

My ranch has a name? Trace explained that the property had been called that ever since he could remember, and with that name came a story. "A legend, really." He frowned, thinking. "Or was it a curse?"

"A curse? Ooh! I don't like the sound of that."

According to legend, that ranch must consist of sevens. When you go back, count the rooms, the horse stalls, and the steps. You will notice a lot of sevens. You might even discover some evidence of sevens that others have missed over the years. Who knows? Maybe the legend is partly responsible for the odd things that are happening to you."

"What's that supposed to mean?"

"When you and Rick moved in, you upset the Lucky 7's apple cart by adding two horses, four cows, and six hens. No sevens. Not a one. No sevens equals no luck if you believe in the curse, which most of the old-timers do."

Hannah liked the idea of being part of a legend. A curse? Not so much. To be on the safe side, she could add a chicken; that wouldn't be a problem. Her creative juices flowed with possibilities. She could draw pictures that contained either the number seven or seven objects, and she could easily add four more framed photos or drawings to the three already displayed on the mantel. She would regain the lost luck in no time.

"What are you thinking about? You have a huge smile on your face right now."

"I'm thinking about sevens. Lots and lots of sevens. Come to think of it, my phone number has two sevens in it."

The smile reached Trace's face as well. "True, but it's not quite that simple. There's more to your number than that, though I can't take the credit. I had no control of the phone number you were assigned. Someday I'll explain if you don't figure it out on your own."

His comment provoked a curious frown. "Hmm, sounds mysterious. In the meantime, would you mind bringing by one more chicken when we get back?"

"Okay, on one condition." His look was far too serious for her simple request. "You've got to quit calling them chickens. Chicken is what most people purchase at the grocery store, all chopped up, wrapped in a package, and ready to cook. I'll deliver an additional hen, an animal that runs around, clucks, and lays eggs."

She cringed at his description. "No problem. I'll expect one more hen tomorrow, then I'll have seven."

"All right then. One Rhode Island Red coming up. I'll bring her by. But I'm warning you, if the hens start liking you better than me, the way Lewissa and Oatie do, I may have to take drastic measures."

They laughed and hugged, enjoying the closeness, the warmth of each other's arms. In the next instant, Oatie jumped up and licked Hannah's face.

"See?" Trace said. "That's what I'm talking about. He loves you and wants to be near you. He doesn't do that with anyone else. I want to check your pockets for dog treats."

His fingers tickled their way into the pockets of her jeans, searching for treats that were not there. She practically dissolved with giggles. "Well, then I will do the same," she threatened, flashing a playful smile.

The mutual pocket checking commenced. The resultant maneuvering forced them to the ground, where they rolled around, laughing like children, neither noticing the uneven rock-covered ground beneath them. His jeans fit snugly and presented a challenge she was determined to meet. She found one front pocket empty and pulled a stick of gum from the other. In a back pocket, her fingers felt a smooth, crinkly square that was not a piece of dark chocolate candy or a dog treat – though it certainly held human treat potential.

The sheepish grin seemed out of place on such a strong, tough cattle rancher, but it was gorgeous on him, nonetheless. "Yeah, I brought one of those, though I hadn't planned on using it. On the other hand, I like to be prepared for anything." He squinted slightly at her, grinning. "Do I detect a brighter shade of pink on your pretty cheeks?"

FIFTEEN

"Show me the inside of the cabin," Hannah suggested, changing the topic of conversation for the moment. Anticipation of the possibilities, the inevitable, lingered in Hannah's thoughts – thoughts she wanted to savor in the privacy of her own mind a little longer.

After Trace used a bit of muscle to pull the rustic door open, they picked up the cooler and the duffle bags from the small porch, entered the rustic cabin, and took inventory of Rosa's handiwork. The woman could whip up meals like no one else.

They found a white bean casserole; a peach and pear, sunflower-sprout slaw; and a variety of cheeses and crackers all ready to eat, no cooking required. However, they would need to build a campfire later to roast the marshmallows needed for the Mexican s'mores.

On the porch, they devoured Rosa's delicious dinner. No high-tech, uptown restaurant could have approached the cabin's unique rustic ambiance or the sunset's magnificent light show that danced on pink and purple clouds. With the setting sun came a sudden drop in temperature, making Hannah shiver. Without a word, Trace jogged back to the Ranger, retrieved a blanket, and draped it over her shoulders. Then he built a warm, crackling campfire.

As he tended the fire, she admired his strong, broad back, and thought the tranquility of this place, with this take-charge, handsome man, seemed too good to be true. Once again, she felt like a princess in a fairy tale, albeit a Western fairy tale. The thought of Cinderella in glass cowboy boots and satin jeans was a fantasy she'd gladly be a part of. The delightful vision produced a soft giggle in her throat.

Trace glanced up. "What?"

"What do you mean?"

"Unexplained giggles are not allowed up here." He winked. How was she supposed to resist that? "So start talkin' ma'am."

She giggled again. "I was just, uh, wondering what Mexican s'mores were made of."

He shook his head, not buying her answer, then

headed inside to retrieve the ingredients for the special dessert Rosa had packed.

"The difference is slight, but I think you'll agree they are extra good." He laid out some cinnamon-coated graham crackers, regular marshmallows, and squares of extra dark chocolate. He handed her a roasting fork, a stick really, complete with a marshmallow attached to its end.

The cooking was fun, but the eating was the best. Hannah had consumed s'mores on several occasions in her lifetime, though none of those compared to tonight's delicious tasty treat. They finished up their fireside snack just in time. A storm cell had rolled in while they'd been eating and with it came plenty of rain. They ran for the shelter of the cabin; Oatie was already waiting on the covered porch.

The one-room cabin had a pull-down double bed, a sink with a pump handle instead of a faucet, and some planks attached to one wall that Trace referred to as "shelves." Two uncomfortable, straight-backed chairs and a tiny woodstove took up the remaining space. No electricity or running water existed – though there was a small, curtained off area in the corner barely hiding a toilet of sorts. She'd checked on that when they'd first entered the cabin. What woman wouldn't?

The darkness of night was fast approaching. Trace

added a glimmering glow to the room by lighting the woodstove and his family's ancient oil lamp. Warmth of a different kind washed over Hannah as she watched him pull down the bed, then cover it with a bottom sheet and two wool blankets.

He glanced over his shoulder, first at her and then at the dog. "Come on, Oatie. Let's take our business outside and give Hannah some personal space."

At first, she didn't comprehend his meaning, then she got it. This was the last call for a private, indoor bathroom break. She stared at the thing in the corner and wondered if it came with directions. Fortunately, she managed to figure it out before man and dog returned.

She peeked out from behind the thin partition and noticed Trace had undressed for bed. She, too, stripped down to almost nothing.

"Won't we be cold?" she asked, her arms crossed in front of her, knowing she was already chilled.

"Well, you know what they say." He cocked one eyebrow, looking solemn and wise. "Naked is the warmest way to sleep when a room's temperature is cold." He nodded with confidence. "I'm pretty sure that's true."

She studied his guileless expression, thought for a moment, then returned a look, a daring look of her own. As he watched, Hannah pulled off her white camisole, then reached down and slipped off her silky white lace panties. When she looked up, Trace was already on the bed, just as naked as she was.

He blinked, bringing himself out of a blissful-looking trance, and then produced a small bottle of champagne, seemingly, out of nowhere. The tiny bottle opened with a festive *pop!* He offered her the first sip. Gently pressing her lips against the rim of the bottle, she tipped her head back. Bubbles ascended upward, tickling her nose.

"Do you like it? This is my favorite champagne." He reached for the bottle and took a swallow.

"It's delicious and cool, with just the right amount of bubbles." Hannah hesitated. "But I'm surprised you brought it here. After what you shared about your father, I thought this might be an alcohol-free zone."

"It used to be. I changed my mind about that today."

After two more swallows, the bottle was empty. Trace cupped his hands around the lantern's chimney and blew as if blowing out a candle, leaving the flickering flames from the woodstove as their only illumination. It was just enough.

"I have a question," she said softly.

"Ask away."

"Is the door locked?"

He smiled, his teeth gleaming in the firelight. "You, my lady, are full of surprises. Rest assured, we are safe behind this door. Any intruder would have to use some real muscle to enter. Besides, Oatie will warn us if anyone or anything comes near, and I have my gun beside me on the floor. Now I have a question for you. Tell me about that pretty necklace I've seen you wear once in a while. Is it special to you?"

"Well, it's a locket. My mom gave it to me the night I graduated high school. It's got a crack in it now, though. The first time I spoke with Lewissa, I must have dropped it in the dirt, and she stepped on it."

"I'm so sorry. I'll gladly replace it for you."

"Thanks, but no thanks. It's fine the way it is." Hannah put the locket to her mouth and blew on it, which produced a faint whistling sound. "And it wasn't the horse's fault. I'd asked her a question, and she gave me an answer with her hoof."

Trace was speechless.

Hannah had another question. "Are your jeans beside you on the floor too?"

"Nope. I hung them on the chair right over there. See?"

"Oh," she murmured, slightly disappointed.

A smile lifted the corners of his mouth. He tilted his head, watching her with a teasing glint in his eyes. "But the contents of my pockets are close at hand."

"Oh!" She felt the heat of embarrassment and pleasure blend on her face. "So, on the floor with your gun is some gum and—"

"And a promise to make love to you safely, gently, and completely."

Trembling slightly, she slid her arms around his neck and surrendered to his caresses. When his hand slid across the plane of her firm belly, a faint whimper escaped her lips. When that hand journeyed a little lower, she froze briefly. His touch had taken her breath away.

"Would you like me to stop? There are no rules about lovemaking up here. Of course, they were never needed before." He stroked the side of her cheek and kissed her nose.

Desire conquered her apprehension. "No, don't stop. Just, please, be patient. This is new for me, and I feel… I feel like I'm losing control." *Not to mention the flips and cartwheels my heart is doing.*

"Good. I'm a patient man, and we've got plenty of time," he said, tickling her neck with his lips and moving his warm hand slowly up the inside of her thigh.

Her breathing quickened with anticipation as she whimpered and moaned.

"You are so beautiful," he whispered.

"I love your touch, your scent, your everything. Even your dog, Oatie," she whispered back.

At the sound of his name, the dog made his own whining sound and jumped up on the small bed.

"Down boy, not now."

Hannah giggled; Trace did not. But they held each other until the rhythm of their warm, naked bodies moved as one. She welcomed the approaching loss of control and – when the time was right – passionately gave herself to this kind, sexy cowboy.

SIXTEEN

Hannah awoke to the smell of coffee cooking over an open fire. For a few moments, she lay quietly on the rustic bed, reflecting on the past twelve hours. She felt so good, so at peace, so... *feminine*. She'd reached a significant milestone; the carefree girl had become a full-grown, desirable woman. She had no regrets. Hopefully, Trace didn't either.

Looking up, she saw him standing at the door wearing only his half-zipped jeans. One hand held a cup of coffee; the other gripped a large towel. He grinned, and Hannah's concern faded away. No one could fake a smile like that.

"Let's go take a dip," he suggested.

Her jaw dropped. "A dip in that ice-cold lake made from melted snow? Please tell me you're joking."

"Can't do that. But I'm not talking about the lake.

There's a small hot spring about two hundred yards to the west, and it's big enough for two, as long as the two sit extremely close together. Believe me, it's worth the walk. After that, we can pack up and head home. I don't want Rosa to worry."

He was right. The spring's hot water both relaxed and soothed her body and mind. She melted into the security offered by his strong, welcoming arms and encircled his waist with her legs. Real-life never felt so good.

THEY'D BEEN GONE LESS than twenty-four hours. Giddiness swept over Hannah as they turned into her driveway. Perhaps, she really could do this: run her mini-ranch, become an artist, grow an herb garden, *and* be Trace's woman. Did she dare have such an ambitious dream? Or was she setting herself up for disappointment with her idyllic thinking? Time would tell.

Lewissa trotted into view, showing signs of anxiety. Something was wrong. She ran back and forth along the corral fence, whinnying, her tail lifted like a flag. Trace stopped the Ranger near the corral and hurried to the tack room for a halter. Hannah searched her pockets, hoping to find a peppermint treat for her horse.

It did not seem feasible for the horse to act this way

merely because they'd been gone overnight. Lewissa had been used to running free in the pasture with the herd for many days and nights at a time. And, she remembered Trace's words – *animals like time alone without humans.* Trace haltered the mare and spoke reassuringly in her ear. He walked her trying to calm her as much as he could, but the tension lingered.

Oatie must have sensed something out of the ordinary too. He dashed around the corral, then the perimeter of the house, with his nose to the ground like a bloodhound at work. Was it the presence of danger or merely something interesting?

"Trace, what's going on? What does he think he smells?"

Trace lifted his shoulders, looking helpless. "I have no idea. Possibly a bear walked through the property, or some other predator paid us a visit. I can't think of anything else that would rile up the animals like this."

Hannah didn't quite buy his explanation. Something about his words and his expression was off. She insisted on checking the hens and found they were all present and accounted for. Next, she headed in the direction of the lower pasture, north of the house, to count all four cows.

"Let me do that." His old-fashioned, protective qualities rose to the surface. Trusting him, she agreed. "I'll take the Ranger down there in a few minutes," he said. "Why don't you go inside and unpack?"

"What, you don't think I could handle a bear?" she asked saucily, lightening the moment. "I'd just sing loudly and add a few intimidating music video dance moves. That should scare off just about anything."

"I feel safer already." His charming smile said everything. "Still, humor me. Until we figure this out, please confine your talents to the house."

On tiptoes, she kissed his cheek. "Spoilsport." Then skipped toward the house and up the stairs, counting each one. There were seven.

The key had been stowed in her sock, but when she balanced against the door to retrieve it, the door swung open on its own. She toppled back and ended up sprawled on the floor. *What in the world?* She'd locked the door; she was certain of that. Had a bear tried to break in? Standing once again, she peered closely at the exterior side of the door and its lock and saw no damage, no claw marks. There hadn't been a bear. She picked up her duffle bag, thinking if a thief had been inside, he'd be sorely disappointed. She owned nothing of value.

As soon as she entered the house, her bag fell to the floor, and a weak scream escaped her mouth. The meager contents of the drawers, cupboards, and closets were now scattered across the room. She collapsed to her knees.

Trace was by her side before she could rise to her feet. She clung to him, and he held her tight.

Fury hardened his voice. "Darlin', I will step up my investigation and get to the bottom of this, right now." Carefully, he helped her up and instructed her to stay close behind him. His fingers closed around his gun as they searched every inch of the house's interior. They found no one.

When she spoke, her voice faltered. "Who would do this to me?"

Trace had no answer but called Rosa to let her know they had returned and what they had discovered. He asked if she'd come over to help Hannah put the place back together.

"Shouldn't we call the police?" Hannah asked.

Trace scanned the room, thinking. "Maybe later. Let's see what we can figure out first."

They searched every room again, looking for clues, but after an hour, they came up with nothing. Luckily, the soda in the fridge had been spared the violence, so they grabbed a couple of cans and took them out to the back porch. In silence, they sipped the cold, sugary liquid – though, at that particular moment, nothing was sweet. Hannah, anxious to begin the cleanup process, held off at Trace's request.

That's when it hit her. She jumped up and raced back

to the living room in search of her only treasured items. She found two of the framed pictures on the floor, each with cracks in the glass, but the third could not be found.

"Trace." She stood at the doorway, puzzled. "The photo of Rick is gone."

He frowned up at her. "That's odd. I'd meant to take a closer look at that."

"Well, I can't find it, and so far, that's the only missing item." She shook her head. "This makes no sense. Who would take the time and energy to trash the entire house, then take only the photo of Rick?"

A vision of Callie's face popped up in Hannah's mind. The teen hated her, wanted her gone, and was jealous of the time she spent with Trace. She'd made that perfectly clear the first time they'd met. She might have created the horrible mess just for the thrill of it. And then took Rick's photo on her way out to add to Hannah's misery.

Not wanting to upset Trace, she shared her hypothesis as gently as she could. "I think Callie might be our vandal."

His blue eyes darkened like thunderclouds, and she saw the line of his jaw tighten. Was it her accusation or the situation that set off this look of rage? Either way, he swiftly resumed his usual, steady-as-a-rock disposition and tightened his arms around her.

"I will fix this, Hannah. This and everything else." He

kissed her forehead. "You're right about Callie playing a part in some of the recent mischief, but I don't know about this latest crime." Looking around, he shook his head slowly. "It reeks of something more sinister."

Rosa arrived and immediately rushed to Hannah, greeting her with a big, motherly hug.

"You poor thing. No one deserves this." First, her eyes scanned the mess, then she blew out her breath. "Let's get going. It'll be fun. We'll clean and organize and make a shopping list as we work."

Seeing that Rosa had things under control, Trace announced that he had business to attend to – Hannah knew the *business* was Callie. Oatie was under orders to stay with the women.

"Mr. McAllister, would you please bring some dinner back from town?" Rosa's happy, calm demeanor reduced the tension in the air. "We will be starving by then, and neither of us will feel like cooking tonight."

He tipped his hat. "Yes, ma'am."

SEVENTEEN

He found her in the bunkhouse wearing clothing that was far from ranch appropriate. Of course, the boys in town would definitely approve; they rarely saw the townies in anything but jeans. Young, female skin was hard to come by around here, a sight for sore eyes, but Trace was above falling for her seductive antics. That's what he told himself.

He hadn't knocked. Why should he? This was his bunkhouse. Callie was merely a temporary hired hand, albeit the sheriff's daughter. He tossed the nearly naked girl a blanket.

"Wrap up. We need to talk."

Laughing, she stood, letting the blanket drop to the floor. She came closer to him, her long legs striding like a runway model. Trace took a deep breath, then stepped heavily to the door, propped it open with a chair, and sat. He refused to play any of her games. He'd had enough of her bad behavior and wasn't about to let her set him up for trouble.

With the door open, nothing blocked the entry of the chilly afternoon breeze, which brought the scantily clad gal to her senses – at least with regard to the temperature. With reluctance, she retrieved the blanket and wrapped herself up.

"What do you think you're doing, Callie?"

"You know exactly what I'm doing," she purred. "And you want me to do it. I just don't know why you insist on playing hard to get with me."

"You're wrong. Totally wrong. What happened to the cowgirl I used to know? The girl in jeans and a tank top? Where'd she go? And what's with all the new duds? Can't come cheap. Been moonlighting? Stealing?"

She scowled. "Yeah, well, what's up with all the stupid questions? I don't have to tell you anything."

"Nope, you don't. Let's take a drive into town and have a chat with the sheriff. Bet she'll get you to answer a few of my questions. Bet she'll ask a few of her own too."

Something like a growl rose from her throat, and she narrowed her eyes. "All right. You win this time, but only because I don't want my mom involved in our romantic problems."

"Problems, yes. Romantic? No! No such thing exists, Callie. It never did, and it never will." He glared at her and, for once, she didn't challenge him. "You *will* answer my questions."

He asked them carefully. Callie was evasive with her answers. Her words so convoluted, so mazelike, that what should have taken ten minutes took over an hour. Eventually, she admitted to doing a few favors for a guy she referred to as Buddy, saying he was a generous guy who paid her well.

"What kind of favors?"

Callie scowled and took her time as if searching for an answer. "Easy stuff. Errands mostly," she said, her annoyance obvious.

"Where's Buddy staying?"

"Don't know, don't care. He's not my type." She glanced away from Trace for a few brief moments. Looking back, she batted her lashes and turned up the heat with her seductive purring. "But you are. You always have been."

He ignored her and continued with his questions. "Give me a few examples of the errands you've done for him. From the looks of your new wardrobe, it appears he's kept you busy. Been spending a lot of time away from the ranch?"

She didn't take the bait.

His eyes stared at her as cold as steel in the arctic. "No problem, your mother will be all too happy to check out the new guy in town. I'll get my answers one way or another."

"How many times do I have to tell you to keep my mom out of this?"

"As many as it takes, I guess, but right now, I'm running out of time. Anything you want to tell me before I go?"

"Where are you going?"

He gave her a confident, knowing smile. "To town."

"Ugh!" The half growl twisted into a half whine. Not a pretty sound. "Okay. Okay. I snipped a wire and stole a stupid photo. What's the big, damn deal?"

Faster than the blink of an eye, the blanket slipped from her shoulders and landed in a lump by her bare feet. Somehow her tiny bits of clothing had vanished. *How the hell did she manage that?*

"Are you happy with me now?" she asked, giving him a sexy pout. "I did as you asked."

He stared. What guy wouldn't? How often does a man see two naked, young women in less than twenty-four hours? He snapped out of his unwanted gaze quickly, angrier than before.

"So you snipped wires, broke into Hannah's place, and stole a photo because Buddy wanted you to?" he asked with stone-cold disgust. "In case you didn't know, those actions are crimes. So, Miss Carter, pack up your stuff and move back in with your mother. You're fired. And if you ever set foot on this ranch or the Lucky 7 without my permission, I will get restraining orders against you. Got it?"

She didn't shed a tear or utter a word, but her hateful glare was impossible to miss. He watched her pull on a pair of shorts and a tank top before pitching all her belongings – including the telltale shoes – into a bag and stomping out the open door. Trace headed off to town.

HANNAH HAD BROUGHT SO few possessions to the ranch that the cleanup would not take long, especially with Rosa's assistance and expertise. With only the kitchen left to organize, she stood in the living room for a moment, staring at the mantel, thankful that the photo of her mom and her drawing of Lewissa had been spared. She made a mental note to purchase new glass the next time she went to town. The missing photo of Rick could not be replaced, and that fact triggered sadness in her heart and an angry, ominous feeling deep in her belly.

Rosa encouraged her to go out and get some fresh air, saying she'd gladly finish up in the kitchen. After all, that was Rosa's favorite room in any house. Hannah dropped several peppermint treats for the horses into her pocket and headed to the corral.

Both horses loped toward her. Clark nibbled the treats from Hannah's hand with his gentle, velvety lips while Lewissa waited patiently for her turn. Hannah had come to love the corral and its horsey aroma. With Trace's help, the area was mucked daily, keeping it pleasant and clean for the horses.

"How was your day, my friend?" Hannah asked the mare. "I wish you could talk. You saw who was here causing trouble, and it was obviously someone or something you didn't like."

The horse bobbed its head, ate one more treat, then trotted across the corral and stopped at the gate. Glancing back, she stomped the ground with her hooves. Hannah got the message. Lewissa wanted out.

"All right, but we need to put your halter on first."

She'd never haltered a horse before without Trace's guidance, but she managed. Halter in place, she attached a lead rope, and out they walked. Lewissa followed politely, stopping now and then to take a bite of grass or graciously accept a scratch between her ears.

Hannah sniffed the air noticing another scent, one she didn't recognize. *Scent* was too nice a word for the noxious stink. Old sweat? Maybe. Tobacco? Probably. Trace didn't smoke or chew tobacco and his scent was always pleasing to her – even after a full day on the range.

Perhaps this odor came from an injured animal, or worse, a dead one. Then again, she thought the smell of recent death would be stronger and make her gag. She'd never been in the vicinity of a carcass, though, except for — No! She would not think about that today. And this smell was different somehow. More *rotten*.

Hannah and Lewissa headed down to the northern, lower pasture where the cows were grazing. The smell of cows wasn't as pleasant as the scent surrounding the horses' corral, but with only four cows in this twenty-five-acre spot, it wasn't bad. Nothing like the odor she'd noticed closer to the house. After a few words with her cows, Hannah turned and led Lewissa back up the hill.

Halfway there, the awful stink rose up again, stronger than before. Had the direction of the wind changed? Hannah hesitated. She was curious, but her gut gurgled, and her throat gagged – definite warning signs. It could be as simple as a dead raccoon, she assured herself. Smelly, but harmless. Lewissa wasn't the least bit curious. Her nostrils flared, and she stomped her hooves, backing up and snorting.

"All right," Hannah murmured. "We'll go home a different way."

Was the horse protecting her or simply emulating the tension surging through her body? Either way, their wondrous connection seemed to grow stronger with each passing day. Releasing her new best friend into the corral, Hannah returned to the house.

"I'm back, Rosa. I didn't see Trace's truck. He hasn't returned yet?"

Rosa frowned slightly. "No, but Harry called looking for him and—"

"Who's Harry?" She hadn't heard that name before.

"One of the full-time ranch hands," Rosa said. "He's kind of a loner, but he's a great cattleman. Does twenty times the work of that loser, Frank, who was here for a few weeks." She smiled to herself. "Even little Callie outworked that man."

Little Callie? Hannah scowled inwardly. How could Rosa describe that curvy, man-hunting snake with such cute and innocent words?

Rosa looked uneasy as she dried her hands. "I think I'd better go see what Harry needs. You don't mind, do you? Trace should be back any minute."

"Of course not. I'll be fine, and thanks for your help."

Oatie tilted his head, his eyes shining. *I'm staying*, he seemed to say.

Saved from the task of preparing dinner, Hannah decided to sketch Oatie.

By the time Trace arrived, she could see the North Star twinkling in the graying sky. Both Hannah and Oatie greeted him with an abundance of enthusiasm before he had a chance to set his packages down. The tantalizing aroma of Chinese food filled the air.

"Hey! I missed you, too, but don't squash our dinner." He laughed and wrapped one arm around Hannah, then placed a quick kiss on her lips. "I brought you something, Oatie. Have you been a good boy?"

Hannah held up the drawing she'd almost completed. "He's not only been a good dog, he's also been the perfect model."

"I'm impressed with both of you."

She set their places at the kitchen island, trying hard not to notice the fresh, meaty bone he'd given to the dog. Looking proud, Trace pulled out a selection of meat-free dishes: vegetable egg rolls, vegetable stir-fried rice, sautéed snow peas, and Buddha's Delight. He was so kind and thoughtful. Hannah was falling for him. No. She'd already fallen, hard. She couldn't imagine a day without him. Was it love? *Am I in love?*

"How was your talk with Callie?" Not that she

wanted to bring the teen into their dinner conversation, but she did want reassurance that all was well.

"Would you mind if we had that discussion a little later? Nothing to worry about, but I do have some news." He looked around. "How was your time with Rosa? Looks like the two of you got everything in order. Is that why she didn't stay for dinner?"

Hannah agreed to postpone the Callie talk. "She left because someone named Harry called, and she decided to go help him."

Trace's expression fell with concern. "Is that all she said?"

"So Harry exists? I thought she might have made up the phone call so you and I could dine alone."

"Well, I wouldn't put it past her. She ought to be called Rosa the Matchmaker. But yes, Harry exists. He's my top hand." Then Trace reached into his pants pocket and pulled out a sheet of paper. "Thought I'd deliver this in person so I could see the look on your face when you see the discount." His eyebrows wiggled with mischief. He handed her a sheet of paper.

A brief sensation of uncertainty swept over her. Why would he smile like a Cheshire cat right now? She began reading the words, even the backside, searching for understanding, waiting for the punch line. "What *is* this? I don't get it." The paper was an invoice addressed to Mr.

and Mrs. Rick Johnson. Hannah felt certain the look on her face was not the one he'd expected.

"I was in town, so I stopped in to say hello to my property manager before picking up dinner. He had this month's bills ready to go out, and I told him I'd deliver yours. You know, save a stamp. Besides, you'll see I made a special adjustment." His charming smile returned, and though it seemed to have lost its effectiveness, he continued. "Rick had sent a cashier's check for the first month's rent. The second month's will be due in a few weeks and—"

"Let me get this straight. You are here to collect the *rent* from me?" Her voice took on a shrill tone loaded with shock and disbelief.

"No, I'm not here to collect anything. You can mail it in. Why are you so upset? I even took off the charge for leasing my animals. I thought you'd be happy about that."

"I… I can't believe what I'm—" The floor seemed to sway beneath her feet, and she struggled for balance. "I don't understand. The Lucky 7 isn't my ranch? Lewissa isn't my horse? Everything here belongs to you?" She trembled. "No. That's impossible. Rick bought a ranch and two horses with a substantial amount of my lottery winnings. The cows and chickens – I mean hens – were the only part of the deal that surprised me. He did his research. He took care of almost everything."

Her new world, her ranch world, had given unexpected purpose to her life in the brief time she'd been here. But it was all a deception unraveling like a ball of string caught on a lizard's foot. Nothing was as it seemed. Hannah, suddenly short of breath, felt herself slipping into darkness.

When the muffled buzzing in her head faded, and she regained focus, she saw two sets of worried eyes, one blue, one brown, staring down at her. Trace's warm hand brushed against her cheek.

"Welcome back."

Oatie licked her elbow, and she absently stroked his head. When she began to talk about these new, disturbing circumstances, Trace put a finger on her lips.

"We'll work this out," he said, tenderly. "For now, I think you should take some time, get your bearings and your strength back. Then we'll talk."

He made some tea. They sipped and sat in awkward silence until Trace finally asked, "So Rick led you to believe he'd purchased this ranch?"

Hannah nodded. "Yes. That was the plan."

"I assure you, he didn't. I can have my attorney make copies of the lease agreements if you can't find the originals." His eyes held hers. "Hannah, I would never lie to you."

She picked up the invoice, needing to see it again, to

know it was real. The fact that it was addressed to Mr. and Mrs. Rick Johnson sent her mind spinning, and she lashed out.

"You led me on all this time," she snapped. "No wonder you came by so much. Just a landlord taking care of his investment."

He kept his voice calm, but she heard a distinct edge to it – an edge he had no right to have. She was the injured party here. Not him.

"I did not lead you on. Rick is the one who deceived you, not me."

"Oh, sure." Her voice was anything but calm. She was losing it. "It's easy to blame the dead guy."

"If he really *is* the dead guy. We don't know for certain that it was his body in the burned car. Remember?"

Hurt twisted in her chest, and panic threatened to take over. When tiny sobs bubbled up her throat, she dropped her head onto her hands and let them come.

"Why don't you call your mother?" Trace suggested, sounding helpless. "Isn't that what women do when they're upset?"

Vigorously resenting his words, she lifted her face and glared at him. "I can't. She's on the move again."

He'd revisit her odd comment another time. For now, he continued his explanation. "My attorney drew up the papers according to the information Rick supplied. I'm sorry, but this is your old friend's doing, not mine."

"Don't try to wiggle out of this."

"Out of what?" He stood, hands in the air. "Hey, I'm trying to be helpful, but I don't need all this drama over a simple invoice. Come on, Oatie. Get over here," he snapped. Trace backed toward the door and stepped outside. "Who are you? I don't even know your real name."

The door slammed shut.

"It's Hannah Langford Hudson," she shouted, tears streaming down her face.

EIGHTEEN

Trace liked a challenge as much as the next guy, but he wasn't up to tackling the impossible tonight. Hannah's reaction had been over the top. Ridiculous. Verging on crazy. He didn't need that in his life.

He hadn't kissed a woman in what, five years? And that relationship had been one manipulative, emotional rollercoaster ride after another. He'd sworn off women back then, and he shouldn't have made an exception now. He'd been blindsided by Hannah's beauty and her vulnerability, but after tonight's irrational blow up, he was over that.

All he needed was his horse, his dog, and his ranch. Not a woman. Plus, this one was complicated. And it seemed she came with way too much baggage.

Now, if only he could stop thinking about her. He hit the truck's accelerator, driving too fast for his own good. Oatie whined, but Trace stared straight ahead, reliving the last few moments he'd spent with Hannah. She'd really pushed his buttons. How could he have let his guard down, been so stupid? At least tonight's reality check had come in the nick of time.

Then Oatie whined again, and Trace remembered. During his angry exit, he'd yelled at his dog. That was a first. The dog had looked warily at Hannah, at Trace, then back at Hannah, obviously reluctant to leave.

Hannah had shouted something too. Had she yelled out a name, her name? He'd been in such a mind-numbing rush to escape the emotional turmoil, he couldn't recall.

As he drove, second thoughts, even regrets, seeped into his brain. Still, he attempted to protect his heart. But why hadn't he left Oatie with Hannah? It was the least he could've done. The dog provided her with the comfort and the protection she so desperately needed.

THE FAINT LIGHT of dawn nudged away the evening shadows from the room, but Hannah still felt enshrouded in darkness. Hoping to distance herself from a bad dream that felt so real, she shuffled into the bathroom to brush her teeth. Looking up into the mirror, the face of the nightmare stared back. Smeared mascara darkened the puffiness surrounding her tired eyes.

It hadn't been a dream. This ranch, her home, did not belong to her. Neither did lovable Lewissa. The worst memory from last night's bombshell was how she'd ranted and raved, wrongly placing the blame on Trace. He'd been good to her, and she'd been unreasonable.

She reached for the phone and dialed his number, oblivious to the early hour.

A sleepy female voice answered. "Hello?"

"Who is this?"

Hannah heard the voice sigh heavily. "It's me, Rosa. I'd just fallen back to sleep. Thank goodness Trace returned to the ranch last night. Harry and I were in dire need of his help. Somehow, the gate to the horse pasture opened; that never happened before. Trace rounded up the horses, and Harry rigged the latch so not even a tornado could blow it open." She sighed again. "Then Trace kept me up the rest of the night talking about the situation. He feels terrible, hon. He had no idea you thought you owned the property. He'd been happy that you, the new renter, cared so much for the place and the animals."

"It was a shock," she admitted, "and I overreacted. May I speak with him?"

"He's not here. Left a little while ago and didn't say where he was headed."

"But I must apologize! I said some hasty, hurtful things."

Rosa reminded her that Trace was a smart man. As long as he was surrounded by wide, open spaces, he'd come to his senses and work things out with her.

Hannah hung up and immediately tensed, hearing a noise outside. She peered out the window and noticed Lewissa tossing her head and trotting from one end of the corral to the other. She performed a sixty-second makeover on her dreary face, pulled on a pair of jeans and the pink hoodie, then went out and stood briefly on the front porch, observing the horse's behavior.

From beyond the end of the driveway came the sound of an approaching vehicle. The horse stood still, listening, and seemed relatively calmed by the noise, but not Hannah. Trace's truck headed toward the house, filling her stomach with butterflies. Was he still angry? Had he come to evict her?

He stepped out and leaned on the truck, hesitating. Seconds later, he turned and strode in her direction. She had no idea what he was thinking. Nevertheless, she ran to him. He reached for her, lifting her off the ground and holding her tightly against his strong, firm body. They kissed, then blurted out simultaneously, "I'm sorry!"

He tipped her chin upward and held her gaze. "I never should have left you last night."

"I should have tried to stop you."

"I came up with a plan," he said hoarsely, drawing back a little. "Want to hear it?"

She nodded, so he took her hand, and they walked to the bench by the corral. The horses ambled over, curious, but today Hannah only had eyes for Trace.

"Our current situation is complicated by an abundance of incalculable factors."

She nodded and smiled sweetly. "Today you're sounding more like a college boy than a cowboy."

He tilted his head slightly. "I once was a college boy."

"Really? What did you major in? Cows?" Hannah laughed.

"I'll have you know, young lady," he said, looking indignant, "that I received a Master of Science degree. I am also a licensed veterinarian." His pride-filled smile became a mischievous grin. "And I like classical music!"

"Well then, Mr. Full-Of-Surprises, let's get back to your plan."

"Let me preface the divulging of my plan, my four-part plan, with one important caveat."

She giggled. "Okay, okay. You've made your

educated point. Now go back to being the cowboy I love."

That last word hung precariously in the air. Her hand flew to her mouth, and heat blazed on her cheeks. Had she really said that? From the stunned look on his face, she must have.

"Okay, then. Moving on." He grinned, giving her a little wink to put her at ease. "You cannot say *no* to my plan until: #1 We've figured out if Rick is dead or alive; #2 If a murder occurred, who did it; #3 Where the lottery money you let Rick play with ended up; and #4 Why Callie is doing favors for a guy named Buddy. Our list of mini-mysteries is a long one. And while we explore all those unsolved crimes, yes, crimes, you'll be my guest, not my renter, at the Lucky 7."

His eyes reflected the calm, peaceful blue of a perfect sky. "And I love you too. Any questions?"

She stared at him, so entranced she could barely think. Finally, she managed to say, "Who's Buddy?"

"A guy, a drifter, who asked Callie to snip your phone cable and steal Rick's photo. And who knows what else he hired her to do. He paid her well for those nasty little deeds. And just so you know, I fired her. I also threatened legal action if she ever set foot on any of my Colorado properties."

Hearing this new information, Hannah found herself at a loss for words.

Trace glanced toward the corral. "Do you feel like taking the horses for a walk or a ride? They need to get out and stretch their legs."

"Oh! I was going to tell you what happened yesterday, but then we got off track. Lewissa was acting anxious again, so I took her for a long walk."

Trace smiled like a proud papa.

"What?"

"You. You're learning fast. I assume you haltered her and attached a lead rope."

"Of course." She shook her head. "By the way, you do know that no matter what the papers say, I am going to pretend Lewissa is my horse, right?"

"Figured as much."

"Anyway, we walked down to check on the cows, which were all present and accounted for." Then she went on to describe the smells and the horse's reaction.

"The rotten smell is probably just a dead, decaying animal: a rabbit, a raccoon, or possibly a coyote." He thought for a moment. "But the sweaty, tobacco smells concern me. Sounds like a human, one Lewissa does not approve of."

Trace decided they'd ride to cover more ground and, hopefully, find out if there had been an intruder, a poacher, or merely a misguided camper on the property. They saddled up – Hannah rode Lewissa today – and headed due north. Oatie followed along.

They passed through an open area dotted with small groves of aspen and then entered a deliciously scented pine forest. Every breath thrilled Hannah. She requested they dismount and let the horses do as they pleased for a while. She wanted time to gather as many pine needles as her pockets could hold.

"Why would you want to do that?" he asked, looking slightly skeptical.

She breathed in deeply. "Why? Never in my life have I lived among pine trees. Until today, I didn't know what I was missing."

She filled her pockets, then Trace chuckled and offered his. She shook her head. As much as she might enjoy trying to shove a few needles into his snug pockets, that endeavor wouldn't add much to her fragrant collection. He pointed at the pouch attached to his saddle, and she nodded. That would work.

Pockets and pouch full, Hannah asked, "Are we still on Lucky 7 land?"

"We are. If we go a little farther, I can show you the northern boundary. For now, we'll just walk the horses through the forest. It's easier."

His words brought a sense of relief. She couldn't

imagine maneuvering around so many tree trunks and branches while sitting on the back of a horse.

"Twins!" he suddenly exclaimed, startling Hannah.

"Twins?"

He grinned. "You and Lewissa. You look like twins with your delicate, golden bodies and your pale, creamy manes. A horse with that coloring is a palomino."

"And what do you call a human with that coloring?"

Without the slightest hesitation, he said, "Too beautiful for words."

Hannah's smile returned, brighter than ever. "What about Clark? He's mahogany-colored with a black mane."

"He's what we call a bay horse."

She was completely charmed by today's horse lesson and continued to ask questions as they walked. Eventually, they reached the remnants of a road, though all that was left were some barely visible dirt tracks. Soon after that, the terrain became rough, rocky, and barren and reminded Hannah of a cold and creepy, post-apocalyptic wasteland.

"This is the end of the property," he told her. "Several old, dilapidated mineshafts still exist up here. If I owned this parcel, I'd fill them in so they wouldn't pose a danger to anyone or anything."

NINETEEN

"Hey, Trace. Let's go home. Can we check out the disgusting smell tomorrow?"

"Absolutely. And with any luck, it'll be gone by then."

Back at the ranch, the cupboards were nearly bare. Trace got a kick out of watching Hannah stare at the emptiness and attempt to come up with something worthy of the title *dinner*. She glanced back at him, raised her eyebrows, and shrugged.

"We could drive into Stillwater," he suggested, though doubted that would happen. She looked exhausted. Oatie was already sawing logs and trotting around in doggy dreamland. "Or I could whip up a trail dinner."

"What's a trail dinner?"

"Anything edible that is fixed by cowboys out on the trail." He grinned. "So what's your pleasure, ma'am?"

"I don't know. The trail dinner sounds a little risky, but going to town for dinner would be like going on a date."

"And what's wrong with that?"

She hesitated, likely thinking about her reply. "Nothing. I didn't think you'd want to do that quite yet. Plus, I want our first date to be special, not a desperate need for food." Leaning back against the kitchen counter, she added, "Besides, I don't have the energy to fix up for a trip to town."

"Hannah. You're beautiful just the way you are. You don't need any fixin' to be town-ready."

"Thank you," she said, giving him a sweet smile of gratitude. "Still, I'd rather take my chances with your trail dinner."

Twenty minutes later, Trace spooned their dinner into bowls as Hannah poured sparkling water into paper cups.

"This is good!" she exclaimed, tasting the meal. "Better than good. What do you call it?"

"Doesn't have a name of its own. It falls under the trail dinner umbrella."

"All right." She chewed the concoction slowly, deep in thought. "I'm going to call it Cowboy Spaghetti. It's spaghetti mixed with, what? Black beans, spinach, onions, and something red?"

Their dinner disappeared within minutes, right along with the light of day. Clouds moved in, blocking the light of the quarter moon, and a welcome hush enveloped the ranch like an early blanket of snow. Trace, feeling content, set out to walk the perimeter, check the horses, and make a quick call to Rosa to ensure all was well. He craved an uneventful evening and a good night's sleep with Hannah by his side and Oatie at his feet.

He scanned the silent darkness once more from the vantage point of the porch, filling his lungs with fresh air. He loved being at the Lucky 7. Of course, Hannah contributed greatly to that feeling, but so did the history of this place. When he'd turned eighteen, his father had surprised him with a box wrapped in colorful paper and topped with a blue bow. Inside that box, he'd found the deed to this section of the family's Colorado ranch property.

From that day forward, the ranch was officially his, and so was the responsibility. Filled with pride, he remembered that day well; the day he'd become a real rancher, his own man.

Something crashed inside, jarring him back to the present. He rushed toward the unexpected noise and into the bedroom. He found Hannah kneeling on the floor, picking up the pieces of the broken bedroom lamp. Oatie stood at her side with his head hanging down. Trace realized instantly what had happened.

"Uh, yeah. I forgot to mention that *fly hunter* is one of Oatie's self-appointed vocations." He scowled at the dog. "One that I do not encourage. Sorry about that. You never want to be between him and anything that flies."

He went to the kitchen for a trashcan and the whiskbroom. Upon his return, he noticed Hannah still on the floor staring at a small object in the palm of her hand.

She held it up to show him. "I thought Jane checked in here."

Sitting cross-legged, she waited for a reasonable, sensible response. He had none. Someone was still up to no good.

"She did," he said. "I think it's time we give the sheriff another call."

"Why would anyone want to bug my bedroom?" Her eyes widened. "Callie! Of course."

Trace didn't want to rush to judgment, but Callie sure hadn't been doing herself any favors lately. "I don't know about that. I made it as clear as a cool drink of water from a Rocky Mountain well that she was never to set foot on this property."

"Since when does she follow directions?"

"Good point."

"Wait. Jane called these short-range bugs. Doesn't that mean the listener has to be relatively close to hear anything we might say?"

"Yeah. I think so." He paused in thought at the troubling implications. "You and I are going to stay together day and night until these odd little mysteries are solved, and every loose end is tied up tight if that's okay with you."

It was. "So where will this togetherness occur?" A mischievous look danced in her pretty green eyes. "Your place or – your other place?"

How should he answer her teasing question? "Your call."

"I'd rather not leave the animals alone."

"We could bring the horses with us to The Big Mack, then come by here every day to check on the others. You will be safer at the ranch with Rosa and me."

He could tell she was thinking. He'd learned to recognize that ponderous expression and wondered what direction her thoughts would take her this time.

"Will we still be able to live, love, and wear our detective hats at your place?"

"With regard to the hats," he searched for the perfect answer, "we must keep them on at all times, but you can wear as much or as little as you like when it comes to the rest of your body." He winked.

I'm getting clever and talkative in my old age.

"Got something in your eye, cowboy?"

Maybe I'm a little premature about the clever part.

Smiling, she held out a hand, and he helped her up. "Let's talk about it in the morning. For tonight, I think we should just settle in right here."

Moments later, they slipped between the bedsheets and pulled up the covers. Even the inside temperature was uncommonly chilly for this time of year. Trace made a mental note to check the propane tank's fuel level in the near future. In the meantime, he rolled her over and pressed his chest against her back, holding her close.

"Trace?" she whispered.

He swept a handful of her silky blond hair over one naked shoulder, then tickled his fingers across the smooth, cool skin of her neck. *God, she's beautiful.*

"Hmm?"

"Sometimes, I get an uneasy feeling – as if I'm being watched. And when that happens, it seems to coincide with Lewissa's anxious behavior."

He stalled, not wanting to share his thoughts on that subject. Starting tomorrow, she'd be safe at the main house.

"Trace? Did you hear me?"

"Yes, darlin'," he said softly. "It's possible we have a

peeping Tom who now wants an audio track to enhance the visual."

"Or a Tomasina!"

He huffed out a breath and draped his arm over her. "Honestly? I can't picture Callie involved in such an elaborate scheme."

"She does have a partner in crime."

"True, but what's in it for her?"

"Money from Buddy and the opportunity to scare me just enough to go running back to Phoenix. But what's in it for Buddy, whoever he is?"

After a few moments of thoughtful silence, it occurred to Trace that there was one major point they'd yet to discuss.

"Hannah, who knows about your lottery winnings?"

"Just me, Rick, and a few people at the bank. Why?"

"Money and greed can turn even a good person toward the dark side. Are you sure your money is in a safe place? Our peeper could also be a thief, or worse. Like I said, folks will do crazy things for money. Especially for a lot of money."

Sleep took a long time coming.

OATIE SAT up straight at the side of the bed, puffing dog breath onto his master's nose. As soon as the man's eyes flickered open, the dog hopped up and positioned himself between Trace and Hannah.

"Hi, Oatie. I suppose you want to go out." Trace leaned over the dog and bestowed a tempting kiss on Hannah's lips. "We'll be right back."

The energizing, early morning air prompted thoughts of yesterday's problems, all of which he planned to solve today. He walked halfway down the long drive, Oatie by his side, his mind racing a mile a minute. Why hadn't Jane gotten back to him regarding the bugs she kept in her desk? Had any of them been missing? He didn't think keeping track of listening devices should be that difficult.

Upon his return, Hannah greeted him with a steaming cup of coffee and a sweet kiss. Oatie's morning meal waited in his dish.

"What's the plan for today?"

Setting his coffee on the counter, Trace wrapped his arms around her from behind and nuzzled her neck. "This. This is my plan."

She turned, smiling. "Good plan. I approve."

"Later on, I'm going to town. I want to have a talk with the sheriff and catch her off guard with my unexpected visit."

"Why?"

"I have a hunch she knows more about the accident, the bugs, and Callie's latest tricks than she's sharing with us. Of course, I could be completely wrong. Maybe she's just lost interest in the accident, or it has come to a dead end."

One way or another, he'd find out what she knew.

"I'll be back in less than two hours with a horse trailer attached to the truck," he said. "Be ready to roll. It's moving day!"

TWENTY

Trace found Sheriff Jane Carter in her office, just as he'd expected. She wasn't sitting at her desk but rather pacing anxiously, a mug of coffee in one hand.

He turned on his magnetic charm. "It's a little early in the day to overdose on caffeine, don't you think?"

She glared sideways. "I'm just trying to stay awake and figure out where my daughter is. Since she's no longer sleeping in your bunkhouse, I expected her to be at home, but she didn't show up last night."

"Sorry, Jane. I understand your worry. Doesn't she have a cell phone?"

"She does. So she's either out of cell service range or choosing not to answer my call. She can be difficult, you know?"

"Oh, yeah. I know."

Jane stopped pacing, set the mug down, and took a deep breath. She folded her arms and squinted at Trace. "What brings you to my office this morning?"

"I missed seeing your smiling face."

"Uh-huh. Right. What's the real reason?"

"Aw, Jane. We're friends, remember?" Her skeptical look said she wasn't buying it. "Okay, I wanted to check with you to see if any new developments regarding the accident had surfaced."

She sighed. "Coroner sent off the best samples of the vic's remains to Denver for analysis. They don't consider our need-to-know a priority, so it may be another week or more before we have a report. Odds are the dead guy is Rick, don't you think?"

Trace shrugged, not giving anything away. "Yeah. Still, it would be nice to know for sure. And the odds are that foul play is involved, don't *you* think?"

"Maybe, but I'm not convinced of that yet. I need proof."

He folded his arms, mirroring her stance. "Would knowing that he'd recently placed several million dollars in an account in Phoenix help you consider the possibility?"

She blinked. "It might."

"Good." *She didn't even know that?* He hid his annoyance behind a smile. "Then I am asking you to take a closer look at the accident using all the fact-finding, detective tools at your disposal. Hannah and I are pretty sure that Rick – let's say it's Rick until we know otherwise – was injured, maybe even murdered, before the car went over the embankment, crashed, and burned."

Her stare was as hard as flint. "And you are just now telling me all this?"

Trace hesitated. "It was just a hunch, and we didn't want to impede your investigation or overstep our bounds."

The officer on front desk duty poked in his head. "Sheriff Carter, there's a guy out front demanding to speak with you. What should I tell him?"

"Tell him I'll be there in a minute." She turned back to Trace. "This won't take long. Help yourself to coffee."

He quickly filled a Styrofoam cup with coffee that he didn't want, then took a subtle look into the top drawer of Jane's desk. The plastic bag containing the first two bugs she'd taken from the Lucky 7 was there, but not much else. He glanced into the other two drawers but found nothing of interest. Where else would she keep them? Hadn't she said similar bugging devices were in her top drawer?

He was standing calmly near the window, sipping coffee, by the time she returned.

"Everything okay?"

"Yeah. Just a guy trying to sweet talk me into ripping up his speeding ticket." She shook her head, annoyed. "Now, where were we?"

"I was about to ask you about the bugs you found at the ranch. Remember? You'd mentioned you had some like that here in your office, and you were going to see if any were missing."

"So you want a bug report? Okay. Listen well because I'm only going to say this once. All the devices were right where I expected them to be."

He hadn't expected that answer. "Are you sure about that? All six?"

She nodded affirmatively.

"So the two from the ranch weren't yours?"

After a negative shake of her head, she said, "Hey, I've got more important things to do than lie about a few low-grade listening devices."

"Did you dust the two from the ranch for prints?" She rolled her eyes. "Good grief. No."

"Here's another listening device that turned up after you'd searched the house. You might want to add it to your collection of bugs waiting to be dusted." Trace didn't try to conceal his frustration or his sarcasm.

"Okay, okay," she said, resigned. "I'll do some dusting, but not today."

Disappointed and more than a little annoyed, he smiled and shook her hand. "Thanks, Jane." He widened his eyes, feigning forgetfulness. "Oh, just one more thing. I'd be grateful if you'd do a little snooping on Lyle and Linda Langford."

"Why? Thought I'd heard they moved to Golden about twenty-five years ago."

"They did, but I think Hannah said her middle name was Langford. I want to know if there's any connection. I vaguely recall they had a teenage daughter back then, but that's all I remember. I was just a kid myself."

"I'll bet you a pizza nothing will come of my snooping. The odds of finding a connection there would be about as slim as winning the lottery."

That made him laugh. "Ah, ha! But people do win the lottery; Hannah is living proof of that. I'll bet you two pizzas and a pitcher of beer that you'll come up with something."

He touched the brim of his cowboy hat, then left her office employing his best, rich-rancher walk. Didn't matter what Jane told him because he would do his own checking on the Langfords if necessary.

But the fact that Jane had not been honest about the bugs was troubling. *Why would she lie to me?* Was she hiding something or simply protecting her wayward daughter from an unlawful entering charge? At least he'd been able to make a little headway in convincing her to push for the identification of the crash victim.

Enough investigating for now. *Hannah, baby, here I come!*

His ranch phone rang, jarring him from the thoughts and visions of his gal. His gal, he liked the sound of that. He rarely received calls on that phone. Only his parents, Jane, Rosa, and now Hannah had the number, and they seldom used it.

"Trace here."

"The bunkhouse is burning up!" Rosa cried, sounding hysterical. "Hurry! Harry and I need help."

He would have preferred more information but, with any fire occurring this late in the summer, time was of the essence. He made the 9-1-1 call.

"Fire at The Big Mack! Send a truck ASAP. I'm headed out there now."

He stomped on the accelerator, determined to arrive in record time. Members of the area's volunteer fire department would likely show up too late to save the bunkhouse; but with his help, they might prevent the flames from spreading to other buildings.

MONSTERS, HORSE MAGIC, FAMILY, & LEMONGRASS

TWENTY-ONE

Hannah had mixed feelings about this move to the main ranch – The Big Mack, as Trace sometimes called it. How long would she stay there? Would this new living arrangement bring them closer together or pull them apart?

Either way, she wanted to be ready when he returned from town. It took barely twenty minutes to pack up a few items of clothing and her art supplies. She carried the suitcase outside, letting the door close quietly behind her, then set it on the front porch near the steps.

Trace would be back soon. The thought curled her lips into a smile, and her body tingled with memories of the night before. Then, she remembered the two precious pictures still displayed on the mantel. No way could she leave them behind. After taking a deep breath of the fresh mountain air, Hannah turned to go back inside the house to retrieve them.

She froze, terrified. What the hell was that? Breathing hard, she spun away from the frightening vision, pressed her back against the exterior wall, and wished she could make herself invisible. She tried desperately to think clearly despite the paralyzing fear that surged through her. Was she hallucinating? Imagining? Had there really been a *face* peering through the top glass portion of the door? How was that possible?

Breathe. Think.

No. That made no sense. She'd just come from inside the house moments ago. Surely she would have known if someone had been there. The back door. Was it locked? She couldn't remember.

It was just my reflection. An optical illusion. She hoped her positive thoughts were correct. Still, they did little to stop the sweat from dripping down her face or keep her heart from beating like a bass drum on uppers.

Bravely, she turned her head and looked up at the door, hoping to see nothing – no such luck. The face was still there, its eyes and nose covered by a black mask. All she could see was a mouth, twisted into an evil, maniacal grin. *I'm losing my mind.* This was nothing like a minor dizziness or feeling faint. This was different in every way as if she'd been poisoned or drugged.

She screamed and turned to run, but a hand clamped her arm tightly and spun her back around. Her eyes blurred with fear. She blinked and stared directly at her attacker. The mask no longer covered his face, and she saw him with abrupt clarity. She screamed again, struggling wildly to escape. This could not be real.

Rick? Oh my God!

Her vision darkened, and she slumped briefly to the wooden surface of the porch. Her semi-conscious moment gave the man just enough time to tie her hands and jerk her upright.

"What the—"

"We're going to have a little talk," her captor informed her, shoving her down the seven unlucky steps.

Where was Oatie? Why hadn't he barked?

"This can be short and sweet," he continued. "If I get what I want, I'll be on my way." He shook her, forcing her to look at him. "On the other hand, this could turn into one hell of a sad and painful day for you. It's already been painful for the dog, but even that could get a whole lot worse."

"What have you done?" The mere thought of Oatie being harmed both enraged and energized her at the same time. She struggled harder to break free.

He seemed to enjoy that. His unshaven face rubbed against her ear. "You're sounding more like a college boy than a cowboy," he taunted, quoting her. She choked on his disgusting breath, thick with the stink of cigarettes.

Rick didn't smoke. Who is this evil man?

"Should I go on? I've got a lot more where that came from."

"Shut up!" she hissed. "Get away from me. Trace will be here any minute. And then we'll see who's sad and hurting."

"Ah, yes. Your beloved cowboy. Oooooh! He's so hot." He chuckled darkly. "No, I wouldn't count on him today. He's a bit overheated right now."

What the hell did that mean? She had to stall, hold him off long enough for Trace to get back. But time was running out. She knew that. This beast of a man, this incarnation of Rick, must have been nearby all week, watching, listening. If Trace hadn't been around so often, he'd likely have done far more than spy on her.

"Chitchat over. Where's the money?"

She said nothing but now understood his motive.

"I want your half of the lottery winnings right now," he continued, smiling, "or I'll hang your dumb dog on that tree over there. You can watch him die."

She stared at the man who looked so much like Rick. But it wasn't him. Couldn't be – unless Rick suffered from a split-personality disorder. Was there such a thing? *Wait! The twin!* From the sound of his voice and only slight facial variations, she concluded he might be the twin Jane had mentioned. Of course, Rudy, the elusive twin. He was alive after all. Alive and crazy. Now that made sense. Terrifying sense.

"My half?" she shouted out. "All of that money is mine."

He landed a punch on Hannah's jaw, and intense, unimaginable pain shot through her. Her legs gave way, and she landed in the dirt, dizzy from the impact. She tasted iron as blood dripped from her lip. *Think! Think!* Crying, she imagined, would only encourage more violence, so she fiercely fought that emotion. She had to keep talking, keep stalling.

Trace! Where are you?

"You're Rudy," she declared, steeling herself against the throbbing in her jaw. "You killed your twin brother. Then you posed as Rick and took my money from the Phoenix bank account. Where did all that money go?"

His nostrils flared. "I'll make you a deal. You give me your half of the money, and I might tell you where my half is."

"It's all mine, you crazy idiot!"

He lunged down at her, punching her face again. Hannah's vision blurred, the world spun. By the time she refocused, there was a gun in his hand aimed right at her head.

"Last chance."

"I wish I could give you the money," she mumbled, unable to move her swollen, damaged mouth normally. "But I can't."

His upper lip formed a sneer. "You stupid, stupid woman. This could have been easy. I never wanted to harm you." He laughed. "Just kidding about that, but I do want your money."

He grabbed her by the hair, pulled her to her feet, and pushed her in the direction of the corral. With her hands bound in front of her and his fist tangled in her hair, her limited, fighting-back options failed miserably. Her failure emboldened him, and he laughed as he tightened his grip on her.

"Fine. Have it your way," he said. "If you won't give me the money, I'll bet your rootin' tootin' boyfriend will, especially if he thinks I'll trade you for cash."

Both horses stomped and squealed with alarm, and Hannah prayed he wouldn't hurt them.

"We're going to take a little ride," he informed her.

She assumed he had a car parked nearby, albeit out of sight. "Where are we going? The money is not in any local bank."

"I already know that." Rudy's tone was indignant. "You're the stupid one, not me."

"Where's your car?" She had to stall for time and keep him talking.

"We're hoofin' it on one of your horses. Oh, sorry. I meant one of *Trace's* horses."

She hated that he knew so much about her. Before today, she'd never experienced true hate. Now she even hated the hating. The deadly combination of the fear, the panic, and the hate forced her down a dark, intensely unpleasant path. *Kill or be killed!* She wished she had the gun Trace had mentioned a few days ago. Then she'd have a fighting chance.

"I'll even let you pick the horse. See what a nice guy I am?"

With Rudy at her heels, Hannah collected a halter and clumsily prepared Lewissa for a ride.

"Hurry up! Ain't got all day!"

She glared at him over her shoulder. "If you hadn't tied my hands together, this would already be done."

Rudy paced, kicking at the dirt while Hannah finished haltering the horse and attaching a lead rope.

"Where's the saddle? I need a saddle."

Hannah thought fast. A saddle would not work to her advantage. "Uh, this horse isn't saddle trained yet." *Would he believe her? Was there such a thing?*

"Then get the other horse."

"Well, that one isn't trained at all. He would buck us

right off, but I'll get him if you're willing to take such a risk."

With a growl, Rudy grabbed Lewissa's lead rope and tied her to a post just outside of the corral, and then he yanked a cloth from his back pocket. Before she could stop him, he'd covered her eyes with a blindfold and tied it tightly behind her head. The immediate darkness was terrifying, as were the warm, sweaty fingers now caressing her neck. She gagged, feeling more nauseated by Rudy's touch than she had by the sight of bloody, raw meat.

"Get up there," he ordered.

Having no sight, no saddle, and no stepladder, combined with her bound wrists, made his demand nearly impossible. *Idiot.* He might know a lot about her, but he knew nothing about riding horses, and that might be her only advantage. Eventually, he was forced to help her onto the horse. At first, he grabbed her around the waist and attempted to lift her. She knew that was never going to work. *Idiot.*

"Put your hands together," she suggested, trying to maintain a polite tone. She refused to let Rudy know how terrified she was. "Lock your fingers together. Make a stirrup."

Grumbling, he did, and she placed one foot into his hands. Slowly going through the motion of lifting herself up to mount the horse, she kicked backward with her other foot using every ounce of remaining strength. Luckily, her foot connected forcefully with his face. He cussed in pain, furious, and his hands – her stirrup – were suddenly no longer supporting her foot. She fell to the ground. New pains throbbed as she tried to catch her breath.

Hannah curled into a protective ball, grunting with every kick crazy Rudy delivered to her ribs. It seemed he wanted revenge as well as her money. *Now who's the idiot?* She used this pain-filled moment to slide the blindfold away from her eyes. Spotting a thick chain on the ground by her bound hands, she closed her fingers around it, rolled over, and then swung it at his leg. When it connected, she pulled. Rudy went down hard, his head colliding with a rock. And now he appeared to be unconscious.

The horse bent down, nudging her, and Hannah managed to stand. Then, stepping up on one of the corral's panels, she was able to climb onto the horse's back. Rudy still lay motionless on the ground, his face dark with blood. How long would he stay down?

"Lewissa," she whispered in the horse's ear, "we need to go. Now!"

Still tethered – Hannah had forgotten that one critical factor – the horse tried to back away from the corral.

Rudy, clueless to the proper way to hitch a horse, had made a mistake. The more the horse pulled, the tighter the knot became until it snapped. The frightened horse reared up. Hannah kept herself from falling off by clinging to horse's mane with her fingers.

"Easy girl, easy," she whispered. "You did it. You'll be all right."

The horse took a few steps away from the corral, testing the waters, then threw her head up, squealing. A rough hand grabbed Hannah's arm. Rudy, with a little boost from the bench, had clambered onto the horse, and now, he sat directly behind her. She felt something hard as metal against her back. Was that his gun? His rank odor and his closeness made her cringe. She almost gagged again.

"Ready to go?"

She spat out the words, "You stink."

"Try camping without any equipment for a couple of weeks. Even you, you uppity rich princess, wouldn't smell like a rose. Besides, on a stake-out, you gotta blend in."

Blend in with what? Cow pies?

One mystery solved. The awful smell had been Rudy and his makeshift campground. The man became more repulsive with each passing minute.

Hannah jerked away from his rough, dirty fingers that

grazed the side of her face, but he was persistent. "Can't let you know too much," he said, pulling her blindfold back into place. "There. That's better." He took a breath, straightened, and yelled, "Giddy-up!"

"They only say that in cartoons, you moron."

She regretted her words the moment they escaped from her lips as he slapped her hard across the back of her head.

"You asked for that."

His body twisted and jerked behind her, throwing something with such force he'd almost fallen off the horse. Whatever it was – a hammer? A crowbar? – clanged as it hit another metal surface, likely the far end gate. Then she heard a piercing yelp, and she screamed before melting into tears. She couldn't bear the thought of sweet Oatie in terrible pain, or worse. The hurt went deeper than any she'd ever experienced.

"Shut up, you bitch," he snarled. "Stop your bawlin'. You'll be just fine as long as I get my money. And I *will* get it. Your rich boyfriend will find the money and deliver the goods. When he realizes the danger you're in, he'll be motivated." He chuckled quietly. "Oh, yeah. Now get this horse moving north."

"I could direct the horse a whole lot better if I could see. Do you even know where you're going?"

He grabbed her hair turning her head, then whispered in her ear. "I know exactly where we're going."

Hannah shuddered. "And just where might that be?"

He laughed, then taunted, "That's for me to know and you to find out."

They rode slowly and quietly for about an hour. With the blindfold still in place, Hannah had to rely on Rudy's crude directions. It seemed he did know exactly where he wanted to go. Occasionally, he muttered, "Go to the left" or "Go right" or "Make the horse go straight." By her estimation, if they were still headed north, they must have gone beyond the Lucky 7's property line and the National Forest. The sweet scent of green pasture grass and pine needles had been replaced by the smell of dirt. Plain old dirt.

"Stop the horse. Ride's over." Rudy cleared his throat. "Hannah disappears without a Trace!" he announced, projecting his voice like an exaggerated news anchor.

He chuckled at his feeble joke, then slid off the horse, grabbing the lead rope from her hands. "Uh, uh, uh. Don't even think about removing your blindfold, or—"

Bang!

Hannah gasped at the shocking, piercing sound of his gun. Increased tension vibrated up from Lewissa's body to her own. She heard the mad man shuffling around, muttering to himself, and she began to tremble. This was likely more than the end of the ride; it was the end of her life. A horror movie could not have been more horrible.

She had to do something. As long as she was alive, there was hope. Just days ago, she'd explained to Trace how she could, sometimes, communicate with animals, especially this animal. Today needed to be one of those times. *Purposeful, positive thinking,* she reminded herself. Slowly, cautiously, she leaned down over the horse's neck.

"Lewissa, you need to dump this guy and find Trace," she whispered urgently, repeating her statement into the horse's ear until Rudy yanked her to the ground. She grunted, landing on her bound hands, which pushed painfully into her sore ribs. Determined, she struggled back up until she knelt, stubbornly, by his feet. Through it all, she repeated the words like a mantra in her head. *Dump this guy. Find Trace.*

"Last chance. Where's the money?" he growled.

Before Rudy had tied the blindfold on, she'd seen his face. She knew who he was, and he knew that she knew. Whether Hannah told him about the money or not, he was going to kill her. She understood that.

Then, unwisely, she growled back at the man, "Over my dead body."

"If you insist," he said, his creepy voice tinged with glee. "Elevator takin' you down."

His boot kicked her shoulder, knocking her over, and she felt herself falling, falling, falling. Her screams echoed in the cold, stale air as her body scraped against dirt, rocks, and tree roots, then bounced off planks of rough timber spiked with rusty nails. Finally, she hit bottom, and her world went black.

TWENTY-TWO

Trace screeched down the driveway, cursing all the way. He'd told Hannah he'd be back in less than two hours and it had been over four. She'd be worried, angry, or both.

They'd managed to put out the fire, but the bunkhouse could not be saved. That was the least of his worries right now. On the positive side, he felt his days of wondering what the hell was going on were nearly over. Something in his gut told him, one way or another, this madness would end today.

The moment he stepped from his truck, he knew something was terribly wrong. Lewissa was nowhere to be seen. Oatie wasn't barking.

"Hannah? Oatie?" He dashed up the steps, his boots

touching only two of them. "Hannah? Where are you, darlin'?"

A note wedged in the doorframe, flapping slightly with the breeze, caught his eye. At first, he was relieved, thinking Hannah had left it for him. Then everything changed.

Dig deep for the money and you might get your honey.

The lake's the place we'll end this chase.

Whoever wrote this note wanted McAllister money or Hannah's money. Probably both. He read it again, puzzled. If this was a ransom note, it was written with such ambiguity that the author risked not getting what he wanted. He hadn't even mentioned a dollar amount.

But if he doesn't get what he wants, what will become of Hannah?

Trace figured "the lake" was the one by his rustic cabin where he and Hannah had made love for the first time.

He had the location but not the cash. He'd never asked where Hannah kept her money; he'd never felt he had the right or the need to know. As for his own money, it would take far too long to go back to town, withdraw a large sum of cash from one of his accounts, and then drive to the lake cabin.

He shoved the note into his pocket. Time was of the

essence, but what should he do first, and where was Hannah being kept? His thoughts were suddenly interrupted by the sound of hoof beats pounding the earth. He spotted Lewissa galloping toward the house, glistening with sweat, a look of terror in her eyes.

"Whoa, girl," he said, raising his palms and moving to her side. She pranced around him, her head shaking, her tail lifted, exhibiting high anxiety. *She knows something.*

He hurried to the truck and grabbed his gun and the bag he'd packed that morning. The mare followed, snorting and stomping the ground impatiently. He mounted up, gave her free rein, and let her do the thinking. The horse did not hesitate and took off at a gallop heading due north. He clung to the horse, praying they'd reach Hannah in time. Were they headed to the lake cabin? If so, they had a long, hard ride ahead of them.

Lewissa veered around most of the dense, forested areas but then slowed to a walk and headed into the trees. Fifty yards in, she stopped where several old, pine trees had fallen, and tossed her head up and down. Trace slid off her back, scouted around, and spotted fresh smears of red on the wood. Upon further inspection, he noticed a faint trail of red going off to the east. He took a few quick steps in that direction, apprehension crawling through his gut. But the horse went wild, stomping the ground and snorting with increased agitation. She was determined to continue on in the opposite direction of the blood trail.

Trust the horse. That's what Hannah would do.

With some misgivings, Trace mounted up, and they meandered farther through the trees. At the edge of the woods, Lewissa exploded back into a gallop. She slowed slightly upon entering the rocky, rough terrain of the old, abandoned mining area, but she kept going.

This was not the way to the lake. Why would the horse come here? Trace hated this place. Still, he fought back his own trepidation and pushed forward. He must find Hannah. They were a team, and he loved her more than life itself. The thought of anyone harming her— No! He must not think like that. He had to stay strong. He was a McAllister.

When Lewissa halted, Trace dismounted and watched the horse take a few slow steps in one direction, then another. She paused, then threw back her head and neighed before lowering her muzzle toward a deep hole.

Trace was at her side in an instant, dropping to his knees. "Hannah! Hannah! Are you down there?" His voice echoed in the hollow space of the old mineshaft. No sound, no voice returned his desperate call. There was no way Hannah could get down there. What was he thinking? Then he heard it.

A whistling sound, a sound he'd heard only once

before, arose from the darkness. Hannah's locket. Relief swept over him. She wasn't out of danger, but he'd found her.

"Talk to me, baby. I'm here. Say something. Anything."

"I… I can't get out. My hands are t-tied." She could barely speak. Her faint, hopeless sob floated up to him breaking his heart. "Tried to shimmy… dirt wall… too wide."

"Are you hurt?" What a ridiculous question. Anyone at the bottom of a mineshaft would have plenty of injuries. "I saw blood on the ground about a mile back."

"Not mine. I've got cuts, bumps, and bruises, but I'm pretty sure I didn't bleed much until I landed down here."

"Did you fall?"

"No. I was pushed."

"By who?"

"Rudy. Rick's twin." Her voice dwindled. "Trace? I hurt all over and I'm so cold."

He had his gun – a lot of good that would do right now – and a few clothes, but that was it. Immediately, he tied the clothing together, including the shirt off his back, to make a rope of sorts. He added Lewissa's lead rope and then fastened one end to a dead, sturdy-looking tree trunk. He tossed the other end down the hole, hoping it was strong enough to support her weight, and that she would have the strength to hold on. He soon discovered the makeshift rope was far too short.

"Hannah, I'd better call for help." He cursed himself, remembering he'd left his ranch phone in the truck. "The nearest help is back at The Big Mack."

The first smatterings of rain tapped the ground beside him and a distant rumble of thunder followed. Could the day get any worse?

"Please don't leave me. Rudy might come back."

The missing piece of the puzzle had dropped into place. At least their enemy had a name. Ironically, that guy was not the main problem right now. The approaching storm was, and it could be lethal. This time of year, when it rained, it poured. The old mineshaft would likely fill up with water and create its own mini-mudslide, burying any contents at the bottom of the shaft, including Hannah.

He sat on the edge of the dark, narrow hole, staring down. The shimmy technique she'd mentioned had potential. With his height and strength that might work if he could control his racing heartbeat. Was he man enough to overcome his claustrophobia? If not, an anxiety attack would surely follow, paralyzing him, sabotaging his rescue efforts, and likely killing them both.

He'd soon find out. She was running out of time and this was the only way he could save her.

"Hang on, darlin', I'm coming. Try to cover your head as best as you can. Dirt, rocks, and debris will fall."

Trace dropped his legs into the hole and felt his stomach drop as well. *Take slow breaths*. He could do this. He *had* to do this.

After tugging on the makeshift rope, he convinced himself that it might be strong enough. Bracing his body, he lowered himself into the darkness, vacillating between thoughts of Hannah and reminders to breathe. Clutching the rope in one hand, he searched the wall blindly for footholds and secure nooks for his fingers. Inch by inch, he slid until he'd reached the end of the rope. The shaft became a treacherous, slippery slope, and all he could depend on were his boots, his back, and his now-bleeding fingers.

Breathe. Breathe. I can do this.

Finally, his boots touched the bottom of the dark, damp pit and he dropped to the ground desperate to hold the love of his life. He could barely see her stooped form in the dark, but she reached out to him. He untied her hands and folded her into his arms. She cried out with pain at first, but clung to him, trembling with emotion. At that moment, he needed her as much as she needed him.

The most physically challenging aspect of their survival lay ahead and time was of the essence. Tiny rivulets of rain trickled down the dirt walls.

"You'll need to hold onto my belt." He hugged her, then kissed her forehead. "Don't let go no matter what and try to support some of your weight against the sides whenever your feet touch."

"I can do that. I *will* do that." Her voice was weak, but determined.

"Let's test our method. If it seems to be working, we'll keep climbing."

He reached up, searching for reliable foot or handholds that might support them both. He knew the odds were not in their favor, but he kept that thought to himself. In general, Trace rarely asked for anyone's help. He considered himself an independent, self-sufficient man, but today he prayed for a little divine intervention. *There are no atheists in a foxhole*, he thought wryly. *Or in a mineshaft.*

"You okay?" she asked. "I know about your fear of—"

He cut her off. "Don't even say the word." His heart already felt like it would beat right out of his chest and they had yet to begin their ascent. "Let's roll, uphill."

Halfway up, Trace's arms and legs shook so hard he didn't think he had the strength to go any farther. Hannah struggled, too, panting with effort. The slick dirt walls made their ascent nearly impossible. Still, they battled upward inch by inch, unwilling to give in to the challenge.

"Trace? Something is dangling just above your head."

He'd forgotten about the makeshift rope. Was it strong enough to hold them both? Did he dare lift one of his hands from the muddy wall to find out? Right now, that hand played a crucial role in holding up the weight of two people.

"Grab it!" she cried, sounding energized. "I can brace myself while you check it out."

Trace had always assumed that a second wind was just talk, a myth, but Hannah seemed to have found hers. Her encouragement gave him the energy and confidence to reach for the rope.

"Got it!"

Gritting his teeth, his back and feet braced against the shaft's muddy wall, he worked his way up, one hand over the next, pleading with the rope to stay strong and for Hannah to hold on. They were only a few feet from the surface, their safety, when a portion of the wall gave way. Dirt, mud, and rocks crumbled and fell to the bottom faster than a California mudslide. Only the toes of one foot reached any solid ground, and he suspected the makeshift rope would come apart any second.

TWENTY-THREE

"Lewissa!" Hannah called. The horse must have been close by because her face poked down into the hole immediately. She spoke to the horse, coaxing her to bend down, come even closer, praying all the while that her weight would not collapse what was left of the shaft's opening.

Trace managed to grasp Lewissa's halter, then gave the command, "Back, back," hoping for a miracle and praying that the horse would pull them up those last few feet. In a flash, they lay next to each other on their backs, chests heaving like marathon runners at the end of a race, barely able to move. The rain beat down, soaking them to the skin. Were they dead or alive? The answer came when Lewissa pressed her muzzle against Hannah's nose, making her smile.

"Your horse," Trace said, "brought me here."

"Oh, Lewissa," Hannah whispered, kissing the horse on its big, velvety lips. "You saved our lives."

"I want kisses too."

Hannah's faint giggle sounded exhausted. "Just call her name. She'll be happy to kiss you too."

"That is not what I meant."

Trace rolled toward her and leaned in for his kiss but stopped short when he noticed the blood and swelling on Hannah's battered face. *That bastard will wish he'd never been born when I take him down.* He doubted a kiss would feel good on her wounded skin. For now, he just held her. Carefully. She smelled like dirt and fear and Hannah.

"Now that you're safe, let's go back to my place," he suggested quietly, helping her rise up from the ground. She shook her head. "I'm *not* safe. Rudy made it crystal clear that he'd leave me alone only if you brought the money he wanted. And you didn't. You couldn't."

"I just wanted to find you. Thanks to Lewissa, I did."

Hannah stiffened, then struggled out of his arms. "Oh, no! I almost forgot."

"Whoa! Slow down. What's the matter?"

"It's Oatie. That creep hurt him. Hurt him real bad."

"Then he's our priority," he said, giving her a boost up onto Lewissa's back.

Trace mounted up behind her, and they headed back to the Lucky 7. Though few words were spoken during the ride home, he brought up the subject of guns again.

"Didn't you tell me once that you knew how to shoot?"

"Yes. It's been a while, though. It will come back to me, just like riding a bike, right?"

HANNAH TOOK a deep breath as they rounded the corner of the house and approached the corral. Though her ribs ached and her face stung, thoughts of Oatie lodged at the forefront of her mind.

The dog was alive but not well. They were surprised to see him receiving some sort of aid from Callie. The girl wore extremely short shorts and her ample, perky breasts were barely covered by a skimpy white cami. What the hell was *she* doing here?

All smiles, she opened the corral gate for Lewissa and her riders. "Hi, Trace. Glad you're back. Rosa said I'd find you here, so here I am. Oatie's gonna need a real vet. I've done all I can, but he needs you." She shot a hostile glance toward Hannah and then batted her lashes seductively at Trace. "I need you too."

Trace dismounted first, then assisted Hannah.

Rolling her eyes, Callie shifted her mean-girl mode into high gear. "You look terrible, Hannah. What happened? Did ya fall off the horse? Maybe collide with a tree?" Then she moved closer to Trace and continued her teasing, seductive ways. "Been mud wrestling? I'd be happy to help you out of those muddy, wet jeans."

"Cut it out, Callie. We've had a hard ride and a tough day."

"Trace, come on now. Have you forgotten already?" She tilted her head in Hannah's direction. "I bet your old lady here would like to know about all the mounting and hard riding *we've* done together over the past year."

"Go home, Callie, or I'll call the sheriff. She'll be happy to put you in the back of her patrol car."

The teen stepped up her game, for sure, but Hannah didn't have the strength to cope with it. Not today. Just thinking of Trace with Callie took all the remaining wind out of her already depleted sails. Without a word, she turned and limped toward the house, sick with self-pity. Maybe she'd have been better off at the bottom of that mineshaft.

Once inside, she glanced out the window and watched Miss Sexy Brat doing what she did best. She couldn't help noticing that Trace hadn't convinced her to leave yet.

Trapped by emotion, the concept of fight or flight

flashed before her like a short-circuited neon sign. She simply had no fight left in her, and that left flight as her only option. She found her purse, though its contents had been scattered all over the floor by the earlier intruder. It didn't matter. All she needed right now was her wallet, the house key, the truck key, and a small bottle of water. Items found, she headed toward the door but stopped and returned to the bedroom. She grabbed the small handgun Trace kept under his pillow and placed it in her purse.

On her way to the truck, she picked up the last two important items: the framed pictures that were still on the mantel. She wished she could shoot the lust-crazed, young trespasser in the yard, but, of course, she wouldn't. Rudy, on the other hand, was a different story. He was still out there somewhere, hell-bent on taking her money and her life. If he'd killed once, he'd kill again. This time, though, she had a gun, and she'd be up for that fight.

Callie and Trace were deep in conversation, or was it an argument? Either way, they didn't notice her. Hannah spotted Oatie lying motionless on the grass not far from Lewissa, and her heart broke. She knelt beside the injured dog, carefully caressing his sweet face. At least he was alive.

"Trace will take good care of you, dear friend."

She stood and rubbed Clark's nose, then hugged Lewissa. A lump the size of a baseball filled her throat.

"You're the most amazing animal that ever walked the earth. I will see you again someday, somehow."

Hanging on to her sanity by the thinnest of threads, she ran to the truck, unintentionally alerting Trace. He followed after her, grabbed her arm, and attempted to hold her close.

"Don't go, Hannah. Please don't go. I'm not sure what's going on here, but Callie's lying, making stuff up. It's a vicious, last-resort act she's putting on."

She jerked her arm free and got into the truck.

Trace leaned his head in the window but was forced to pull out as the truck began to move. "He's still out there," he warned, "and he's mad as hell, I reckon. He won't give up, you know! He's in too deep."

She kept on driving, her heart breaking again as Trace shouted his last words of wisdom.

"He's dangerous! And he's got nothing to lose."

NEEDING to be three places at once, Trace wore a path in the grass, pacing, searching his mind for the best course of action. Oatie needed him at the main house, the Sheriff had to be notified of the attempted murder, and – whether she liked it or not – Hannah needed him too.

When Rudy realized his captive was no longer stuck

in the mineshaft, he'd hunt her down. In all three cases, time was of the essence. And then there was Callie. Trace's fury increased with every word she spoke.

"You know you want me," she purred, moving closer.

He shoved her back. "Get away from me." Crouching at Oatie's side, he lifted him gently and carried him to the truck. "You get to ride shotgun today, old pal."

Callie persisted. "I'll go with you. He needs someone to hold him, to keep him from sliding around." She folded her arms, increasing the cleavage already displayed. "I know you're gonna drive fast."

He leaned down, so his angry eyes were inches from hers. "Get this, Callie. I do not want your help. I do not want you around. Not now, not ever." He straightened, hands on his hips. "But I have one question. Why are you here putting on this little show? Why today?"

She shrugged and probably realized she'd been caught. "Just earning some cash before my generous employer has to leave town. You know, make hay while the sun—"

"Your employer is that guy you call Buddy?"

She nodded, frowning slightly. "Poor guy. He had a rough day. I had to patch him up even before I got to Oatie. He was bleeding all over the place, babbling something about an accident. He sure was in a hurry." Then a rare, coy look spread across her face. "Oh, and he finally told me who he was. You are gonna freak out. My Buddy is really *Frank*, your ex-ranch hand."

Trace glared at her, then got in the truck. "Frank put you up to today's drama?"

"Uh, actually, no. Not all of it. It was my idea to stop by today 'cause I heard Hannah might be gone for a while. Then Buddy drove in, all messed up. He asked me to turn up the heat a little if I saw you again. Just to annoy you and keep you occupied for a while." She stepped up to the truck's door and reached through the window touching his cheek ever so lightly. Far beyond annoyed, he shoved her hand away.

"Hey, whatever. I had nothing to lose and everything to gain." She shrugged again. "But yeah, most of the pranks were his idea. It was all pretty crazy, but when he told me who he really was, I figured that he had some kind of grudge against you. You did say he was worthless, and I'm guessing you probably hurt his feelings. So it was payback time." She frowned. "But he had lots of money, so why would he want to work as a ranch hand for you?" She bit her lip and appeared to be thinking about that.

As he listened to her ramble on, a few more puzzle pieces slid together. Rick's twin, Rudy, had likely caused Rick's death and emptied the Phoenix bank account.

Maybe he'd been after Hannah's lottery winnings

from the beginning.

Rick's photo – the one that had gone missing from Hannah's mantel – had always looked vaguely familiar, and now he knew why. Rudy was Frank. No wonder he and Hannah hadn't been able to figure out what was happening. Then he wondered if Callie knew of Rudy's existence or relation to Rick. Or that Buddy, Frank, and Rudy were one and the same?

He didn't have time to spare, but he stayed a few minutes longer because she was still talking, divulging facts that he needed to know.

"I don't see what you're so upset about. She'll get over it and come running back to you. You and Little Miss Sunshine can have great make-up sex in a couple of hours, thanks to me." Her scornful eyes traveled over him, and her attempt at a pouty smile hardened. "You guys were really mud wrestling, huh?"

"For your information, we were trying to stay alive." He narrowed his eyes. "Maybe you've forgotten something, Callie. You're not allowed on any of my properties. Get out of here before I have you arrested for trespassing."

"Someday, you'll be sorry you treated me so badly."

Shaking his head, Trace sped off, kicking up gravel under his tires. One hand was on the steering wheel, the other on his injured dog.

TWENTY-FOUR

Hannah's only motive? To distance herself from Trace and Callie. She couldn't bear the sight of them together. Beyond that, she had no plan. At the end of the driveway, she took a left turn toward town and wondered if Trace or anyone else had been watching her pull out of the Lucky 7.

With bitter tears spilling from her eyes, she traveled about a mile, then turned the small truck around. She drove right past her driveway and headed north. North to nowhere. She didn't want to see or speak with *anyone* right now. She passed the turn-off to the McAllister Ranch and kept going, but she slowed as the seasonally maintained gravel road came to an end. Only vague tire trails, riddled with rocks and ruts, continued beyond this point.

At first, she hesitated, fearful of heading into unknown territory, but then the terrain began to look familiar. Of course! Trace had driven his Ranger up this way when they'd come to his private, rustic cabin by the lake. The cabin would be a perfect place for her to regroup, make a plan, and move on with her life. Trace would never suspect she'd run to this remote area by herself. Certain that solitude was just up ahead, she patted the remnants of her locket and felt safe in a cold, lonely sort of way.

Maneuvering the pickup over and around the ruts and rocks grew increasingly difficult, nearly impossible. Looking ahead, the roof of the cabin came into view. She could walk the rest of the way if necessary – and it was. She'd run over something. The underside of the truck clashed with a rock. A deafening squeal cut through the air, and her transportation jerked to a violent stop. No amount of rocking back and forth brought the desired result. The truck was stuck. Then the engine quit.

The air was so still her ears tingled. Feeling suddenly vulnerable, she unfastened the hood latch and got out to check the damage. Steam rose from the engine, and a yellowish liquid dripped on the ground from the under-carriage of the truck. She hadn't minded the thought of walking the rest of the way to the cabin, but a damaged, non-working vehicle? That was a serious problem. Out of the blue, her mother's words came to mind: *Be careful what you wish for!* Hannah had wished to be alone, far away from everyone. Wish granted.

She grabbed her purse and reached for the two beloved, framed pictures, but decided they'd be safer in the truck. She started to lock the door, then scolded herself for taking such a silly, useless precaution. Up here, no one was going to steal anything from her broken down truck. Trace hadn't felt the need to even have a real lock on the cabin's door, for that matter.

With a heavy sigh, she headed toward the place where she and Trace had fallen in love. The uphill walk from the truck to the cabin took more energy than she'd expected. She'd never hiked this far, especially not at this altitude, or after a day filled with injuries and life-threatening danger. Her lungs demanded more oxygen with each step, and she worked up a sweat despite the chilly temperature.

Finally, she arrived at the only entrance to the cabin. Breathing hard, she put both hands on the handle, her foot to the wall, and pulled using every remaining ounce of strength. The rustic door flew open. Proud of her accomplishment, she stepped inside and came face to face with—

"Rudy! What are you doing here?"

The deranged man's initial look of shock quickly morphed into a surly, smug grin. "I'll be conducting a business transaction any minute. I hadn't planned on a threesome, but I think it will work out just fine. Maybe better than fine."

A threesome? Who else? Trace? *Oh, God. Please let it be Trace.*

Hannah's face and body still pulsed with the pain inflicted by this deranged man, but now she noticed with satisfaction that he had sustained additional injuries beyond the bump on his head.

She couldn't resist. "What happened to you? Did you and my horse go your separate ways?" She should have stopped right there. This man was a killer and wouldn't appreciate any humor, especially at his expense. "Did you have an unscheduled dismount?"

Rudy moved like lightning. He yanked the purse from her shoulder, shoved her onto one of the wooden chairs, and tied her hands tightly behind her back. She groaned, her shoulders screaming with the strain.

"You think you're so damn smart," he hissed. "You're not. You're just a stupid, rich bitch." He rummaged through her purse. "Ah, ha!" he crowed, strutting and waving Trace's gun in the air. "Now I've got two! This day just gets better and better."

Once again, Hannah believed if she kept the psycho talking, he'd be distracted and wouldn't kill her. At least not right away.

"Did you take your brother's photo from my mantel?"

"Nope. But I did see two other pictures when I was on one of my many fact-finding visits. Who's the broad?"

"The broad? No broads on my mantel." She narrowed her eyes. "The *lady* with me in the photo is my mother."

"Ah, Mommy Dearest," he said, as a twisted, evil grin spread across his ugly face. "You should give her a call, invite her up. I'll bet she knows where some of your money is."

"You know there's no phone here. Only Trace's—" She shook her head, noting he'd stopped listening. "Never mind."

Trace's parting words echoed in her brain. *"He's a desperate man with nothing to lose!"*

And now, he possessed her gun. Her only hope was to wait for a chance to get the better of him. If she wasn't the victor today, she doubted there would be a tomorrow.

OATIE STOOD the best chance of survival if Trace took him directly to the vet in town. There he would be x-rayed immediately, treated accordingly, and monitored around the clock. And once the dog was safely there, Trace would be able to focus his full attention on finding Hannah.

After dropping off Oatie, Trace set out again. He scanned the trucks parked on Main Street as well as the parking lots at either end of town and determined she was not there. He pulled over and picked up his phone.

"Rosa. Have you seen Hannah?"

Rosa sounded bewildered. "No. Should she be here?"

"It's a long story, but she's in terrible danger. I can't explain it right now, but if you do see her, insist that she stay with you. Lock the doors and keep a gun handy."

"Oh, *mierda*," she said, her voice filled with tension and concern. "I'll keep my eyes open. Trace, wait. Harry mentioned that he'd seen tire tracks heading north on the trail to the lake, more than one set. He thought we might have trespassers."

Rudy was waiting there for him, Trace remembered, and for the money. "I'll head up that way."

"Be careful, Trace. And hurry back. Two special guests are on their way to the ranch."

He hung up. Guests? This was no time for guests. They'd have to wait. With tires squealing, he headed onto the highway, but within seconds red lights flashed in his rearview mirror. He pulled over, livid. He didn't have time for this, either. Jumping from his truck he met Jane halfway.

She tried to appear serious, but her smirk slipped out. "Sir, do you know how fast you—"

"Jane, I can't talk now. I need you to look the other way just this once. Have you seen Hannah or her truck?"

"No," she said carefully. "And you'd better have a heck of a good reason for skirting the law."

"I do. And it's a matter of life and death. You've got to trust me on this."

Her lips pressed together, then she nodded. "For the safety of all those I protect, I'm giving you a red-lights-flashing, sirens blaring escort to the county line. After that, it's out of my jurisdiction. Let's go!"

They ran to their vehicles, and Jane took the lead. When they approached the county line just past the Lucky 7, she pulled over and rolled down her window.

"I've got some news about—"

"Later, Jane."

Rudy waited for him at the cabin. Had Hannah gone there too? He could think of no other logical reason for the presence of more than one set of tire tracks this far north, unless Callie headed up there after they'd parted ways. That was a concern. If she had gone up to the cabin to warn her employer, she'd have a good head start. But no, that was unlikely. She'd never been to his cabin before... or had she?

Concluding that the second set of tire tracks was more likely made by Hannah's truck gave him a sick, menacing feeling. In his mind, he pictured Hannah struggling to open the cabin's door, then finding Rudy there. At this point, the two of them together added up to a deadly combination, and the crazed twin had the advantage.

One set of tracks veered off the trail about a half-mile from the cabin. A hundred yards farther, just over the ridge, he spotted Hannah's truck off to the right. He parked next to it and decided to walk the rest of the way.

He needed the element of surprise on his side. He also needed his gun, which was usually in his truck. Not today, though. He'd taken it along on his wild horseback ride to find Hannah, and he hadn't put it back. A few tools in the cabin could be used as weapons – a hammer, a wrench, and – *oh, hell* – he'd left the chainsaw there. He hoped Rudy hadn't discovered that.

When he reached the cabin, he peeked in one of the small windows and spotted Hannah right away. She was tied to a chair, her hands bound behind her back. Rudy sat opposite her, pointing a gun directly at her face. Oh, no. He squinted. That was the gun he'd kept under his pillow. She must have brought it with her. Good girl! But now it was in the hands of a madman.

Fortunately, he saw no sign of the chainsaw. Taking a deep breath for strength, he yanked open the door and burst through.

"No!" Hannah shouted, but her warning came too late.

TWENTY-FIVE

The trap Rudy had set wasn't intricate or intelligent, but it was effective. Trace's fast-moving feet tripped over the wire strung tightly across the doorway about eighteen inches above the wood plank floor. He was only down for a few seconds, but Rudy was ready. He jumped the distance to where Trace had fallen and brought his knee down hard on his back. There was a loud crack, and Trace groaned in pain as his chest hit the floor.

"Gotcha now, cowboy," Rudy hissed. "I'm not so incompetent now, huh?" He tied Trace's hands as he had done with Hannah.

Once his captives were firmly secured, Rudy strolled casually around the room, wearing a distorted, fiendish grin. "This is fantastic! You two just made my day. Want to hear what's next?"

Trace ignored him. "Hi, Hannah, darlin'," he said gently. She looked understandably shaken. "You doing okay?"

Her expression was achingly sad. "I've been better." She sighed. "Oh, Trace. I'm so sorry. I never meant to put you in danger."

"Shut up!" Rudy snarled. "Just shut the fuck up!"

Trace glared at Rudy, then smiled, noticing the deplorable condition of his face. He knew now that the blood he'd spotted on his way to find Hannah the first time had belonged to this son of a bitch, and that Lewissa must have bucked him off onto the pile of dead trees.

"Hey, Frank, Rick, Buddy, Rudy. Who are you today? And how'd you get so banged up? No, wait. Let me guess. You performed an equine-assisted aerial maneuver."

Rudy scowled, "What's with you people?"

Hannah grinned. Not a time for laughing, but Trace was glad to see she could still manage a smile.

"Not all that surprising," Trace continued. "You never belonged on the ranch. You don't belong anywhere. Even prison is too good for you."

"Oh yeah? Well, your time is just about up, cowboy." Rudy leered at Hannah. "It didn't have to be like this, you know, bitch. If you'd given me what I asked for, we wouldn't be here. I'll give you one last chance to get me that money."

"I don't have it," said Hannah.

"You're lying. You have *millions* of dollars some-where." He pressed the gun against Hannah's brow, exasperated. "Tell me now, or you won't live to see the moon come up."

Hannah gasped and squeezed her eyes shut, still not giving in.

Trace clenched his fists behind him, and his heart nearly stopped. He couldn't let this happen. If Hannah refused to reveal the location of her money, he'd offer his. "Move the gun away from her head." He spoke calmly, in an emotionless monotone. "My family and I have more money than she'll ever have. I can get you $500,000 in twenty-four hours. What do you say?"

Hannah's eyes opened, damp with tears.

"I say we've only just begun," he sneered, the hard iron of the gun barrel now pressed to Trace's temple, making him flinch. "What do you think, Hannah? What will you offer me if I don't put a bullet in your boyfriend's brain?"

Hannah's emerald eyes locked onto Trace's. He felt the love radiating between them and knew it was solid, unwavering, no matter what happened.

"Love is worth more than money, Rudy. But you wouldn't know about that, would you? You can have it all. Every last penny."

Rudy hooted out a laugh. "Now you're talking. See? That wasn't so hard. Aren't you glad you finally wised up? Just make the calls on that ranch phone you're so fond of, Trace. I'll wait." He stepped back, giddy as a ghoul humming the Final Jeopardy tune. "Times up. Make the call."

"That's going to be a problem. The phone is in my truck."

"Not a problem for me. I know from experience that your truck isn't locked.

The deranged man collected a dozen or so of the longest sticks from the wood box. They watched as he topped those sticks with a few thin towels and secured them with his leftover pieces of rope. "Be right back," he told his captives, grinning. "Don't go away."

His gleeful whistling faded as he got farther from the cabin and closer to the trucks.

"Oh, Trace," she said, still speaking softly. "Even if we could hand over a million dollars right now, he's not going let us live."

He'd hoped she hadn't figured that out. "Yeah, I know," he admitted. "And he's going to be *really* pissed off when he discovers the ranch phone isn't in the truck."

She swallowed. "He's got another gun tucked in his belt."

"Good to know. I'll make sure I get it as soon as my hands are free." He squinted toward the window but saw only darkness. "I reckon he'll torch the trucks. After that, he'll come back and shoot us." He paused, thinking. "We can't allow him to do that."

She shivered, and her lips trembled, breaking his heart. "We're out of options, aren't we?"

Then an idea came to him. "Can you cry?"

"Huh? You know I can."

"Yeah, but can you cry on demand? You know, fake it? Pretend?"

"I've never cried fake tears before, but I'm confident under these circumstances, it won't be difficult to do here."

The other part of his plan was pretty far-fetched, but he decided it was worth a try. "And you know that horse whispering you do with Lewissa? The positive thinking stuff?"

She nodded.

"Does it work on people?"

"How should I know?" she admitted. "I never tried that."

There's a first time for everything, he told himself.

Keeping his voice low, he let her in on his wild plan, admitting it wasn't much, but it was all they had.

Minutes later, Rudy stormed back in, bringing with him the stink of his crude torch and the burning trucks. He hopped easily over the trap he'd set for Trace and then stomped toward Hannah. As planned, she'd burst into tears the second he'd come inside, and that seemed to confuse him.

"Hey, shut up, no crying." Then he jabbed the gun at Trace. "You tricked me. And you're gonna pay for that. Oh, yeah. You're gonna pay, big time."

Hannah intensified her performance, and Trace cringed because he knew her tears were not entirely fake.

"Aw." Rudy drew close to her again, curling his voice into baby talk. "Poor widdle thing. Are you sad because you're gonna die?"

He laughed maniacally, waving his gun in one hand, the torch in the other. The flame passed mere inches from her face.

"No," she sniffed. "Well, yes, but it's not just that. You ruined everything for all of us."

He lifted one dark eyebrow, vexed. "Oh, sure. Blame me. It's not my fault he forgot the phone."

"No!" she cried. "You don't understand! I b-brought the money with me! I knew you meant business, and you'd never give up. My money, *your* money, was in my truck!" She threw back her head, sobbing hysterically. "You burned up two million dollars!"

"Liar!" Shifting nervously from one foot to the other, Rudy aimed the gun at Hannah's chest, then at Trace's head, as if contemplating who to shoot first. "You're lying!"

"No! I'm not!"

His smirk disappeared, and he glanced nervously at Trace. "Ain't true," he tried to convince himself.

"Sure is, Rudy. You screwed up big time. That smell out there? That's two million dollars going up in smoke."

Rudy shook his head, refusing to listen. His crazed eyes darted from one captive to the other, desperately seeking reassurance. The hand holding the gun was no longer steady. It trembled as it moved back and forth from target to target.

Knowing the odds were against them, Trace and Hannah gazed lovingly into each other's eyes. That intimate communication instilled courage and strength, proclaiming endless love. They were not ready to give up. When she nodded, they turned their heads toward the evil man and, like deadly laser beams, stared into his crazed eyes.

Rudy's face held a look of terror. He rocked back and forth, wildly waving his gun in the air. Was that a good sign? Trace wasn't sure, the guy was too unstable to figure out, but they pushed ahead to part two of their plan.

Barely blinking, barely breathing, Trace and Hannah steadied themselves. Using every brain cell at their disposal, they'd bombard Rudy with their mental message.

And so it began: *Rudy ruined everything.* At first, they whispered the words, the mantra, over and over like wicked ghosts, hoping to push Rudy over the edge. But when he cocked the hammer, ready to fire the gun, Hannah spoke the mantra out loud and stomped her feet to the rhythm of the words. Trace joined in. *Rudy ruined everything. Rudy ruined everything.* With each repetition, the speed increased, the volume rose. The tense, explosive energy within the cabin's walls felt unearthly, and the room vibrated like a rocket, ready for liftoff.

Rudy tried to cover his ears, even though his hands were occupied holding the gun and the torch. When that proved to be impossible, he added to the frenzy by screaming, "Shut up! Shut! Up!"

With his expression more distorted, more crazed than ever, Rudy shifted the gun's aim from Trace to Hannah, then back to Trace. He stomped his own feet and continued to shout, "Shut Up!" to the eerie rhythm that shook the room. As quickly as flipping a switch, a strange stillness suddenly took over Rudy's body, his breathing now bizarrely slow. Silence. Without focus or any movement of his head, his dark eyes darted to the left, then to the right. With no one there able to stop him, Rudy lifted the barrel of his gun. Then, in slow motion and with diabolical ceremony, he squeezed the trigger. *BANG!*

TWENTY-SIX

The deafening sound of the gunshot produced an incessant, metallic ringing in his ears. The flash caused temporary blindness, which added to the confusion. What just happened? The grotesque devastation left behind kept any logical thoughts at bay. Trace stared helplessly at Hannah, still sitting upright on her chair, motionless. He wished he could hold her, let her hide her sweet eyes against his chest, but his hands were tied with the strong, rough rope.

"Hannah," he said, hoping she'd respond.

She lifted her face, her eyes filled with anguished emotion.

Trace breathed a sigh of relief. "We did it, darlin'. Rudy's dead, and we're alive."

She nodded but seemed unable to speak. For a

moment, they sat, eyes locked on each other, hearts pounding, waiting for the shock to subside.

Hannah saw it first. Eyes wide open, jaw dropping, she managed to scream, "The cabin's on fire!"

The rich scent of flaming timber reached Trace's nose, and he knew this old structure would burn fast. If only he were closer to the spot where Rudy had dropped the torch, he could stomp out the fire while still tied to the chair. Turning his head, he saw that the flames were already too high for that to work.

With only one option left, Trace scooted his chair across the rough, rugged planks and turned his back to the flames. Taking a quick, deep breath, he steeled himself, then tipped the chair back on two legs, and thrust his hands into the fire, hoping to burn the ropes and free himself.

Was he still glad to be alive? The agony was unbearable. His tortured flesh blistered and bubbled, and a horrific smell filled the air. However painful, his hands were soon free. Clenching his teeth, he fumbled with Hannah's bindings and set her free too.

"Run!" he shouted, but she was already gone, racing toward the lake. He looked back only once, just in time to witness the cabin imploding into a gigantic, raging ball of fire.

TRACE KNELT, dipping his hands into the cold lake water and leaning slightly against Hannah for support. She had escaped without any burns, and although her lungs felt scorched, all she could think about was Trace's agony.

"Trace, what can I do to help you?"

He leaned his head close to hers and gently kissed her bruised and battered face. "Quite a lot, I think."

His voice was hoarse, and though she was tired beyond belief, she knew he had to be exhausted. The sweat brought on by fear and the fire's heat now chilled their bodies. Hannah shivered convulsively but willed herself to find strength.

"T-tell me what to d-do."

"It could be daybreak before anyone realizes we didn't make it home." He gave her a sweet little smile. "Even then, they might figure we got romantic and stayed up here."

"So you're telling me we're on our own?"

"Well, darlin', I think we should prepare for that worst-case scenario and keep hoping for the best."

"What's the plan?"

"You're going to do some digging. My hands are useless."

"All right. With what? And what am I digging?"

"Come on. I'll show you."

He led her along a barely visible path. Suddenly, she couldn't move fast enough. The pungent odor of sulfur hung heavy in the still night air, smelling of hope. In all the confusion, she'd forgotten about the hot spring. She craved its warmth.

"Wait. You need to dig first." Trace pointing at a boulder supporting several sturdy branches she could use as primitive digging tools.

She gazed into Trace's eyes, knowing he saw the fear in hers. "What am I digging?" she asked again.

He blew out a long breath. "I know this will sound creepy, but it's the only way to avoid becoming victims of exposure."

"What? Tell me."

"Hannah," he said slowly, "I need you to dig a shallow grave for two."

Her jaw dropped. "A *grave?*"

"Yes. I guess I should have called it a bed, but who digs a bed?" He cringed at his own stupid words, though 'shallow grave' accurately described what the hole should look like.

Under different circumstances, she'd classify Trace's creepy comment to his odd sense of humor. But tonight, salty tears streamed down her face stinging the open cuts she'd received earlier in the day. Was this how her life would end? Lying in a hole and covered with dirt?

Trace continued to verbalize his plan but tried to conceal the effort and the slowness of his speech from Hannah. "Keep the loose dirt close by. We will remove our clothing, soak in the hot water until our body temperatures rise, then lay in the shallow *bed* using our clothes and the dirt as a blanket."

"I'll hold onto you, Trace, like never before. I'll be your hands tonight and every night until they heal."

He sighed. To finally be so much in love and on death's doorstep at the same time seemed unreal. "Hannah, darlin', we'll repeat that process as often as we need to until the sun comes up. After that, its warmth will keep us alive while we make our next plan."

Hannah wiped away her tears and started digging.

THEY SHOOK UNCONTROLLABLY, worse than before. Another dip into the warm water was long overdue. Hannah was freezing, and other than the involuntary, constant tremor rolling through her, she barely moved. Her slim frame's low percentage of body fat would not sustain her much longer if they didn't get into the water now.

"Let's go swimming," murmured Trace.

"Can't."

"I'm not going without you," he said, struggling up from the blanket of dirt.

Unable to use his burned hands, Trace positioned his upper arms carefully under Hannah's arms and dragged her to the water. The warmth loosened her jaw enough to speak.

"I love you more than anything in this world," she whispered. "And I'm s-sorry."

"For what?"

"If I hadn't moved to the Lucky 7, we wouldn't be clinging to life in a warm puddle."

He sank a little lower, keeping his hands above the waterline. The heat of the pool intensified the pain in his hands.

"True, but if you hadn't, I would not have found the love of my life."

"You're a good man, Trace." She sounded sleepy. "Let's stay in the warm water until morning."

"I don't think we should do that, but I have an idea."

When he decided they'd had enough, he directed her to rip his shirt into two pieces, dry herself first with one, then dry him with the other. His theory? Dry flesh would stay warmer than wet flesh. They nudged back down into their bed of dirt.

Trace attempted to instill a sliver of hope with this minor addition to their process and didn't tell her how limited their chance of survival was. He struggled to stay vigilant, wanting to protect her with his life, but the cold and the day's exertions lulled him into a numbing sleep.

TWENTY-SEVEN

Rosa kept Mr. and Mrs. McAllister occupied with hors d'oeuvres and spiced tea. She cheerfully assured them their son would arrive any minute, but the longer they waited, the more she doubted her words.

"Rosa, dear," Alice McAllister said quietly, "I know you pretty well. I can tell you're worried sick about something. So start talking. Where's Trace?"

Before she could answer, Harry rushed through the front door. "Something's happened, Rosa," he blurted out, too troubled to notice the presence of Trace's parents. She shook her head frantically, hoping to spare them any bad news, but he kept talking. "It's almost dark, it's getting late, and there's no sign of him. And just now, pretty sure I saw smoke billowing up in the direction of—"

"Harry!" Rosa interrupted.

"Oh!" he said, finally seeing the guests. "Mr. and Mrs. McAllister. Sorry for barging in like this."

"Hello, Harry," Clint McAllister replied calmly. "You were about to tell us the smoke's location. Is my son in trouble?"

Harry hesitated.

"Come on," Clint said. "We haven't got all night."

"I don't know the details," Rosa said, intervening for Harry, "but several troubling events have occurred around here and at the Lucky 7. Fires, poisoned stock, fences coming apart, and possibly even—" She stopped, unable to say the word *murder*. She glanced at Harry. "The smoke might be coming from the lake cabin. I think Trace and his friend, Hannah, are in danger. They should have been back by now."

They all experienced the déjà vu of that moment. *They should have been back by now.* Almost fifteen years ago, Alice had said similar words when Clint's return home had been overdue. Now, this small group sat silently, anxiously, watching the patriarch and listening for his comment, his directive.

"Let's get a search party up there." He glared at the little group. "What are you waiting for?"

Rosa ducked into the kitchen. While she gathered

supplies with one hand, she called the Lucky 7 using the other. The phone rang and rang unanswered.

Harry, with the help of two additional cowboys, packed up two quads, the Ranger, and the double-cab truck and trailer with blankets, rope, and lights. Rosa added food, first aid equipment, and warm clothing. Last, they loaded a horse into the trailer, just in case they needed to go where the vehicles could not.

"Hold on! You're not going anywhere without us," Clint stated with conviction.

Everyone turned and stared at Trace's parents. Rosa pleaded with her eyes and a tiny shake of her head, not wanting to offend. No one ever spoke about the wheelchair, but if she had to, she would.

"Oh, Mr. McAllister. I don't think that is a good idea. It's rough going up there. Rougher than it used to be. It's cold and dark and dangerous. And Alice, you've only been out of the hospital a week."

Alice was determined, then Rosa realized what Alice already knew: Clint *needed* to be part of this search and rescue mission.

"Family sticks together," she told Rosa. "That's all there is to it. Clint is just fine, and I'm completely over that awful virus. Now, let's go. Rosa, drive us in our truck. It'll get us there or close. Come on, Clint."

"I'll be right there. I just need to grab something."

TRACE AND HANNAH LAY SHIVERING, shaking, wondering if they'd survive, and questioning if they were even still alive. There was no way of know how much time had passed when Hannah mumbled, "A horse. I hear a horse."

"Mm. No way, darlin'."

"Yeah."

They both drifted off again.

"Trace? Trace!" She shook his arm. "I really hear something."

He heard it too. The sound of an engine – no, many engines. *Likely just a jet high above us*, he thought.

"Look," she whispered.

Lights. Thin beams of light darted all around, bouncing off shadows. Trace thought he heard the faraway sound of a man yelling. *Am I dreaming or hallucinating*? Still, he listened to the voice, trying to make out the words.

"Trace!" He finally heard it. It was real. "Trace! If you're out there, talk to me."

He knew that voice! "Dad?" He struggled to rise, his hands useless and his pain level increasing with each passing moment. Hannah propped him up as best she could.

"Dad?"

"Trace?"

They heard the sound of a high-tech, electric wheelchair coming directly toward them, followed by the crackling of a walkie-talkie.

"I found them!" Clint yelled, his voice choked with emotion. "Alive! Harry, drive my truck up here to the hot spring. Rosa! Bring all the blankets."

Clint's flashlight landed on the couple, temporarily blinding them. Trace blinked up at his dad, at the muddied, all-terrain wheels of his chair, and the expression of obvious relief on his face.

"Oh, Dad. Never in my life have I been so glad to see you."

"What the hell happened here? The cabin is nothing but smoldering timbers, and the two trucks are charred metal shells. Now you're here, covered in mud. Did some psychotic SOB try to bury you alive?"

"The bad guy's in the cabin, and he's dead, Dad. Burnt to a crisp. It's a long, long story."

Clint raked his fingers through his thinning salt and pepper hair, frowning at his son. "So you buried yourself?"

"Well, no. Actually, it was Hannah." He lifted his pitiful, blistered hands. "My hands are out of commission right now. Got a strong pain pill in your pocket?"

His dad reached into one of the storage pouches on his rolling, metal mustang and pulled out a fifth of Wild Turkey. "Been carrying this around with me for almost fifteen years. It's never been opened, but I knew it would come in handy someday."

Trace looked shocked.

"For medicinal purposes," Clint explained. "This'll help."

Hannah took the bottle and held it to Trace's lips.

"You first," Trace insisted.

She took several sips. The unpleasant taste of the whiskey brought on a sudden alertness. Fortified, she held the bottle against Trace's mouth, and he took several long gulps. Rosa arrived with the blankets, and Harry rolled up in Clint's truck. The others gathered around, overjoyed.

A reflective smile spread across Trace's face. He and his dad locked eyes.

"So, this is it, huh, Dad?"

"Yep, sure is."

"The search party payback."

Clint shrugged. "It was the least I could do."

The band of rescuers caravanned through the darkness, illuminated by headlights and a waning crescent moon. Trace and Hannah, wrapped in several wool blankets, silently appreciated each other and the truck's heater though their bodies still shivered and their teeth chattered.

Once they reached the main house and were under adequate indoor lighting, Alice determined their injuries included far more than near hypothermia. She insisted the best doctors in Colorado check them out. Before the sun made its appearance, Hannah and Trace were transported to University Hospital in the McAllister family's helicopter.

Though out of the deadly cold and off the high altitude mountaintop, they were not yet out of the woods.

TWENTY-EIGHT

Two Weeks Later

Hannah glanced around the huge, festively set table, taking in every face, every gesture, and every spoken word. Ever since Trace's parents had moved to the Denver area, a few years after Clint's accident, Trace sat at the head of the table. Tonight, he deferred, insisting that his dad take that seat and his mother occupy the chair at the opposite end, just like old times.

When all but one of the fluted crystal champagne glasses were filled – Clint took his sobriety seriously and prepared to toast with a glass of sparkling water – Trace whispered, "Ladies first," into Hannah's ear. She rose slowly, feeling a bit weak in the knees. There was so much she wanted to say, to share, but tonight was not the time for that. Tonight was a celebration of survival and family, Trace's family.

She lifted her glass and took a deep breath. "To the McAllister family and friends. I want to thank you for your kindness and your hospitality." What else should she say?

Her eyes were drawn to Trace's mother and father. "Thank you for your bravery and for organizing the search party." She took a shaky breath, determined not to cave to the emotion bubbling up within her. "I owe my life to you and to Trace."

"Hear! Hear!"

Glasses clinked, and everyone settled in for the first course, a steaming bowl of lentil-carrot soup. In appreciation of Rosa's dedicated, ongoing service to the McAllister family, Alice had arranged for a chef and his assistant to create the evening's celebratory dinner. She insisted that Rosa be one of the guests tonight. Jane, Harry, and a few of the ranch hands sat at the table too.

Oatie lay on the floor between Trace and Hannah, his tail quietly thumping whenever anyone looked his way or mentioned his name. Callie sat in jail, waiting for her day in court. Jane was not quite ready to post her bail.

Next, Trace rose to deliver his toast, awkwardly

holding his glass in gauze-wrapped hands. He quietly asked Hannah to help him out and lift his glass. She stood up beside him, loving the light in his eyes and the sparkle of his million-dollar smile.

"I want to thank every one of you," he said, his gaze pausing briefly on Jane, "for being here tonight, and for being part of my life." Then he turned to Hannah. "And I want to thank you, Hannah, for showing me the sweeter side of life and for expanding my mind to the intuitive nature of horses. You're my inspiration, my motivation. In case you hadn't noticed," he told everyone else at the table, "we're a darn good team." Satisfied, he smiled. "Cheers!"

Hannah listened in awe to conversations that took place at the dinner table about the ranch, the wildlife, and family. If the truth were known, she was in awe of the dinner table too. The shabby apartments she'd lived in as a child had only small kitchen tables where only two people ever sat. Her mom didn't socialize, so no friends ever came by. That was how they lived.

Tonight, she realized that a critical component was missing from her life. Family! Trace had generations of family to learn from and be part of. She'd had only her mom and their occasional, shallow conversations, although she had to admit her mom came up with some mighty fine words of wisdom now and then. If only her mom would come to the Lucky 7 for a visit, she might stick around for a while.

Bittersweet memories flooded her mind, and her heart ached as she pondered the family dynamics that surrounded her. Did she dare hope to be a member of this family some day? Or was this merely one short chapter in her life's journey?

After dinner, Trace bid Harry and the cowboys good night while everyone else reconvened in the main living room. A crackling fire warmed the air around the enormous stone fireplace. Trace sat opposite the heat on the large leather sofa with Hannah. She snuggled up close to him, her feet tucked under her, wondering if it bothered him to be near these flames.

Holding hands, Clint and Alice sat comfortably on one of the loveseats. Oatie rested his head on Jane's lap, as she sat on the thick, plush rug, leaning back against Rosa's chair. Songs from Zac Brown's latest album pulsed softly in the background.

"Did you tell your dad about Lewissa?" Hannah asked.

"Not yet." He glanced at Clint. "I think Lewissa might have laminitis in her front hooves. I've noticed a slight limp the past few days. Not surprising after the trauma she put herself through with all those wild rides back and forth from the Lucky 7 to the mineshaft, supporting two riders."

"Well, son. You're the vet. You would know. What's the plan?"

"I'll arrange for the farrier to come out and check her hooves, and I'll reduce her intake of sugar and starch, just to be on the safe side."

Hannah listened closely. Before the kidnapping and the horror of the recent days that contributed to Lewissa's new condition, she'd conducted some research of her own and had a plan as well. "I'll rub her hooves with alternating layers of wintergreen and lemongrass oil. I'll also stir up a mixture of coconut oil and lemongrass oil she can lick from my hand."

With looks of surprise, almost everyone turned toward Hannah. Alice spoke first. "Are you sure that's a good idea, dear?"

Hannah nodded.

"Hannah's been studying the use of essential oils," Trace assured her.

When Alice seemed pleased, Trace whispered into Hannah's ear. "Your research includes the use of oils with *horses*, right?"

She gave him a nod and a knowing smile. They could discuss her supplemental treatment plan in greater depth later.

"Trace," Clint started, sounding fatherly. "I know you've spent the past two weeks recovering, but since we're heading home tomorrow, how about a debriefing session while we have you, Hannah, and Jane all together."

He nodded reluctantly. "Okay. Here's the nutshell version." He looked at Jane. "Feel free to jump in anytime." He took a deep breath, gazing at the fire. "I think you all know by now that Hannah won a large sum of money in the lottery. For some reason, her friend Rick falsely led her to believe he'd purchased the Lucky 7 Ranch where they'd intended to live separate lives, following their own dreams. Shortly after their arrival—"

"Within a few hours," Hannah cut in.

He nodded. "Yes, probably within a few hours, Rick died in a suspicious car crash, likely murdered. We now believe the murder was committed by his twin brother, Rudy, who had been secretly spying on Rick and Hannah back in Phoenix long enough to know about her lottery win. Rudy impersonated Rick when he went to the bank, withdrew the money, and closed the account. Apparently, the two million sitting in that account wasn't enough for him. He got greedy and wanted it all." He turned to Jane. "You want to fill us in on what you discovered about the twins?"

"There's not much to tell." Jane hesitated, clearing

her throat. "I learned that Rick was adopted by his first set of foster parents and he inherited the name Johnson, so he became Rick Johnson. Rudy wasn't so lucky. He was never adopted, lived with several foster families until he turned eighteen. Apparently, he took off on his own in search of his brother, but I'm not sure of his motives at the time. We think the twins' biological parents' name was Santana because that was the name most often associated with Rudy. It's more theory than fact, though."

Hannah tilted her head. "Rick never mentioned a twin brother, though he must have known he had one. Didn't you tell us a few weeks back that the boys lived together for the first few years of their life?"

"Again, many assumptions are at play here. What we know is that the boys were placed in foster homes before entering kindergarten. We don't know what their circumstances were prior to those placements."

"That's so weird. Rick had always claimed to have *no* family. Now I'm wondering what became of his adoptive family. Where are Mr. and Mrs. Johnson?"

Jane sighed. "Good question. They could be deceased and had absolutely no connection to the events up here, but I don't know. Rudy found Rick, so I suppose he could have found them if he'd wanted to. He might have caused them harm. It's all speculation. Fortunately, there's no need to know. The victim and the kidnapping murderer are gone. The case will soon be closed."

Clint sat quietly to the side, holding his chin in his hand and tapping one finger against his cheek. "Hold on there, Jane. Doesn't seem to me the case should close just yet. From what I've heard about the past few weeks, several issues are still unresolved.

TWENTY-NINE

Tonight's purpose was one of celebration and family. No one was in the mood to discuss the recent past or solve problems except for Clint. So, he continued asking questions and expecting answers.

"One of Trace's bunkhouses burned to the ground, one of his cows poisoned, and fences and trees vandalized. And then there's Hannah's missing money, which Rudy withdrew from the Phoenix bank." He turned toward Hannah. "Sweetheart, did I hear you say the money in your possession burned up along with the truck?"

She hadn't wanted to discuss her money or lack of money with anyone but Trace, but couldn't ignore Clint's direct question. "Yes, Mr. McAllister. I sent my mom a fair amount of the money at first, to help her out and for safekeeping. I also hid a substantial amount of cash behind the framed drawing of Lewissa, between several sturdy layers of mounting and backing material, until I could get settled and open a bank account here. I'd placed the check I was saving for investment purposes behind the photo of my mom. And, yes, both were destroyed in the truck fire. Luckily, the bank will reissue the check, but the cash is gone."

Jane jumped back in. "We're working with PPD on locating the money Rudy removed from the Phoenix bank. That's one aspect of the ongoing investigation, so I can't comment on that."

Trace frowned. "What became of those listening devices used to bug Hannah's place? You had a total of six in your desk, right? I hope you've figured out by now that three of those ended up at the Lucky 7. Did you check them for prints?"

"Yes, I did, but I can't comment on—"

"Okay, I get that, but no legal rules are constraining my comments, so I think I can contribute a fact or two about those bugs. Callie admitted to placing them at the Lucky 7 at Buddy's request and direction." Trace turned to his dad with a brief explanation of the Frank-Buddy-Rudy connection. "The way I see it, she must have taken at least three of them from your desk, Jane. Or did she take them all?"

Jane gave Trace a blistering glare adding to the tension slithering around the room. Her reluctance was understandable; she was Callie's mother. But, by now, she must have known her daughter was involved in the vandalism as well as the harassment of Hannah and Trace. Questions still remained about the extent of her participation in the crimes of grand larceny, murder, kidnapping, arson, and attempted murder. That was enough to make any mother glare.

"It's an ongoing investigation, Trace. That's all I can say."

As much as she disliked the girl, Hannah hoped Callie wasn't tied to those serious crimes. Jane and Trace had been friends for over a decade. Both would be devastated if Callie's actions destroyed their friendship. Only time would tell.

The more Clint listened, the more puzzled his expression became. "Hannah, something still troubles me. Why would Rick lease the ranch and the animals instead of buying them? You had plenty of money, and the plan was to purchase a ranch, correct?"

Hannah nodded, then frowned, unsure of where Clint was headed with his question.

"I think he might have been in on a scheme to keep a large sum of your money for himself. And then that scheme backfired."

The room got quiet. More than one set of eyeballs glanced sideways. That shocking scenario had not crossed anyone's mind. Trace was the first to speak. "The ranch was not for sale, Dad. So Rick couldn't have bought it, but he should have explained the situation to Hannah."

"Rosa," asked Alice, kindly, "do you have any more of your famous strawberry tarts back in the kitchen? I think we could all use a sweet treat about now."

"Yes, ma'am. Jane, want to give me a hand?" Rosa was also brilliant at defusing tense situations.

"Sure. Why not?" Her tone flat, with no sign of a smile.

As they waited for the tarts, Hannah detected a secretive glance exchanged between mother and son. Before she could question it, Alice stood up and held out a hand to Hannah.

"Let's go outside," Alice suggested. "Rosa will bring the tarts out, and we can look at the stars while we wait. I'll miss seeing them once we're back in Denver's bright lights."

It was a perfect night. The stars twinkled peacefully in the ink-black sky. Contented mutterings of horses and the occasional bellow of a cow were the only sounds heard in the stillness of the evening. The hens had gone to roost hours earlier.

"I'm so glad we had this time to get to know you, Hannah," she said. "And it's wonderful to see Trace so happy."

"He's a kind and amazing man. I'm so lucky to have him in my life. We became close quickly – like a whirlwind." Hannah's line of sight shifted from the sky to Alice. "I wish you could stay longer."

She nodded. "We'll visit soon enough. I feel you're the daughter I never had, yet always hoped for."

A sudden thundering and beams of bright lights cut through the air, startling Hannah. Alice appeared unfazed. In fact, she smiled as if she'd just witnessed a twinkling shooting star. Soon, the loud light show revealed itself as a helicopter, and she squinted upward, confused. The only time Hannah had seen a helicopter here was for their recent medical emergency, but no one needed such transportation now.

Curious, she watched it land. After the rotor stopped spinning, a man and a woman climbed out and hurried toward the house. The dampness of tears glistened on the woman's face, but she was smiling. Hannah looked at Alice, hoping for an explanation, but none came.

"Why is she crying?"

"Why don't you ask her?"

When Hannah asked her question, the white-haired

woman smiled and touched Hannah's cheek. "Tears are in my eyes because this is the happiest day of my life."

Her comment only added to Hannah's confusion. It was time for some clarity.

"Hannah," Alice said, "I'd like you to meet two of my dearest friends, Lyle and Linda Langford." Then she placed her arm around Hannah's shoulders, offering support. "Lyle, Linda, it gives me great pleasure to introduce you to your long-lost granddaughter, Miss Hannah Langford Hudson."

THIRTY

Hannah remained at The Big Mack for another week. Trace had insisted. Rosa added her style of enticement including delicious meals and stories about the ranch's history. While there, she also took the time to process the recent events and come to grips with her family's existence and her own tragic story. Each member of her biological family had made life-changing mistakes. Linda, her grandmother, shared a few of the details before flying back to Golden. Hannah listened and learned.

Alice added what she'd recently discovered. "Lyle and Linda were prominent and wealthy. Their only child – your mother – was the joy and the center of their life. When she became pregnant at the age of eighteen, her boyfriend long gone, their hearts broke, their lives shattered. Distraught, ashamed, and concerned over how their family would be viewed by friends and neighbors in their elite community, they told Lillian to leave and to never come back.

"A few months later, filled with regret, they came to their senses. But, by then, they were unable to locate you and your mother. They tried but failed. It seems Lillian relocated often to increase the distance from the family that had so heartlessly tossed her out. I think she wanted to leave the devastating pain behind and create a new life for herself and you, her baby."

As a young child, Hannah had been well aware of their transitory lifestyle, though she didn't understand the reasons for all the moves.

"Where is you mother?" Alice asked.

"I don't know right now. Since I moved out, she doesn't always tell me her location, but she contacts me about once a month to make sure I'm all right."

Hannah anxiously awaited her mother's next contact, knowing this time, they'd have a lot to talk about.

While driving one of the small ranch trucks back to the Lucky 7, Hannah's mind swirled with thoughts of rebuilding her life and following her dreams. She wasn't about to run back to Arizona, that was no longer her comfort zone. No. She looked forward to remaining on the ranch for the next six to twelve months, and she wouldn't mind if Callie's spiteful prediction – that she wouldn't make it through the winter – proved to be wrong.

Home at last, Hannah took advantage of the warm, mid-September morning and sat on her seven steps ready to create a new to-do list. From this vantage point, she watched her horses and her hens. They were happy. They knew this was their home, the place where they'd be well cared for every day.

Hannah sighed, smiling, and began to write.

Furnish the living room.

Upgrade and organize the kitchen.

Build a small greenhouse.

Purchase starter plants for the creation of essential oils.

Add to pathetic wardrobe.

Draw another picture of Lewissa—draw everything!

Download and print another photo of Mom.

The list might have been longer, but the sound of a truck pulling into her driveway distracted her thinking. Not recognizing the vehicle, she ventured back inside and locked the door. Not that she was afraid, she wasn't, but she was wary. A little extra caution never hurt.

At last, the truck came to a stop, and Trace stepped out. Delighted, she flung open the door and hurried to his side. He pointed to the bed of the truck. There she found hen number seven flapping noisily in its cage, and she quickly let her out. Trace, his hands still bandaged, lifted Oatie from the front seat and placed him gently on the ground. The dog walked with a limp, and his head and sides bore stitches, but his tail wagged just fine.

"Doc, all but promised my hands would heal completely, except for some scarring," he said, leaning down to kiss her lips. "The vet's prognosis for Oatie was encouraging too. His recovery will take longer than mine, but he'll be almost as good as new." He touched her cheek with the fingertips of one hand. "So, please Hannah, smile. That's what we need right now, your sweet and beautiful smile."

Gently, she took his bandaged hands in hers. "How did you drive all wrapped up like this?"

He shrugged. "I borrowed Harry's truck. It's an automatic, so all I had to do was steer. Well, that and drive slowly." One side of his mouth curled up. "Driving slowly was my greatest challenge."

"Oh, Trace," she sighed, snuggling into his arms.

It was nice to be alone for a change, away from the well-intentioned others who had hovered over them at the main ranch for the past few weeks. Today they embraced not out of fear or lust, but love, true love. Hannah closed her eyes and held on tightly, wishing this warm, tender moment could last forever. Then, teasing, she placed her hands on his firm butt and gave him a squeeze. Her fingers met with a hard bulge in one of his back pockets, and her ears heard a faint, crinkling sound coming from the other.

Her eyes opened wide with curiosity. "A bulge *and* a crinkle? Want to tell me about that?"

"No. Not really."

She stepped back, hands on her hips, fully expecting an explanation.

Reluctantly, Trace threw up his hands. "Okay, I give up. Just keep in mind that I intended to save the contents of my pockets for later."

Tilting her head, she bit her lip in speculation. "Which pocket should I look in first? Hmm, I think I'll investigate the bulge."

"Uh, you do realize," he said, straight-faced, "that we're talking about a bulge in my *back* pocket, right?"

She batted her eyelashes. "Maybe, for now."

He laughed, and his eyes sparkled with anticipation. He held his bandaged hands up and out of the way. "Well, you're going to have to investigate the bulge on your own."

His tight pocket clung to its treasure, making her wonder how he'd gotten it in there in the first place, considering his injuries. Her slim fingers wiggled as she struggled to remove the small, velvet jewelry box. Her jaw dropped as she held it up for him to see.

"Uh, huh," he said, smiling. "Go ahead. Open it."

The sun beamed down on a shiny, sparkling ring. It bore diamonds in the shape of a tiny horseshoe.

Hannah gasped. The sight of it took her breath away. "Is this what I think it is?"

"If you think it's an engagement ring, then yes." Hiding her smile, she punched him in the bicep. "Huh!" he said, sounding hurt. "Is that any way to treat your future husband?"

Her eyes dampened with joy, blurring her vision.

"Yes," she whispered.

He grinned. "Yes? That's the way to treat me?"

"No, of course not." She looked indignant until she saw the love in his eyes. "Yes, I would love to be your wife someday."

He didn't look surprised, but the slight relaxation of his shoulders told her he was relieved by her answer. "Good." He placed his bandaged fingers on her waist urging her closer. "How long have we known each other, Hannah?"

"A little more than a month."

"Right. In the grand scheme of life, that's a pretty short amount of time. So here's my plan."

She listened, astonished and pleased to hear he'd been

thinking about their future already. He recommended a one-year engagement period, wanting to adhere to proper wedding etiquette.

"During that time, I'll live in my ranch house, and you'll live in yours." He winked. "But of course we could always—"

"Don't you mean that you'll live in your ranch house and I would live in your *other* ranch house?"

He frowned and shook his head. She'd brought up a subject he'd rather delve into some other time. Grudgingly, he pointed to the pocket that crinkled.

"Help me out here."

She handed him the paper from his pocket, and he immediately handed it back.

"Read it."

Curious, Hannah unfolded the wrinkled, crinkled sheet of paper, but hesitated, remembering the last time he'd given her something to read. *We're engaged now. How bad could it be?* And so she read. Not believing the words, she read them again. Her heartbeat sped up, making her dizzy and her world blurry. She began to swoon, but Trace caught her in time and led her to the nearby bench.

"Catch your breath. I'll be right back."

Her eyes drifted to the paper in her lap as he walked toward the truck. When he returned, her eyes still stared at the words, but she was soon overcome by a musky, sweet scent she hadn't noticed before.

Trace smiled and said nothing. Hannah barely noticed him because her full attention was on the wriggling, whimpering puppy held by his bandaged hands. A baby Oatie!

Trace lifted one shoulder apologetically, then carefully handed her the tiny creature. "He wouldn't fit in my pocket."

"Oh, Trace!" The puppy clambered up her arm, nibbled at the buttons on her shirt, and licked her neck while Trace showered her with his own kind of kisses.

"Uh, I think you dropped something," he said, drawing back a little.

Overwhelmed by emotion, she'd almost forgotten about the sheet of paper that had sent her reeling. Though filled with legal jargon, Hannah understood the document's main points. Not only had Trace given her all of the animals, but he'd also given her, by way of a quitclaim deed, the entire ranch.

"It's all yours to keep," he said quietly. "No strings attached. Not a one." He looked away. "Oh, wait. One small, skinny string does exist."

Her euphoric state of mind flickered and faded just a bit. Deep down, she'd known this was too good to be true.

"Here's the thing," he said, sounding serious. "I can't have my future wife feeling faint every time a murder occurs, she's given a gift, or finds true love. I want you to start growing some of those herbs you've been reading about and turn them into an oil that will keep you by my side and fully conscious. I don't want you to miss a single minute of our beautiful life together."

That was a string she could live with. "Okay." Overjoyed with Oatie at her feet, Trace by her side, and a puppy in her lap, a few happy tears spilled out. The puppy enjoyed the salty taste. As he licked her face making her laugh, one big problem came to mind.

"Trace, I need to change your plan for our wedding. It just won't work."

His face projected pure shock. "What's the problem? Was it something I said?"

"Yes, as a matter of fact, it was. I will not marry you in one year." She could no longer hold back her teasing smile. "But I'd love to be your wife in seven months."

Hannah and the puppy were inseparable from the moment Trace plopped him on her lap. Before the sun set on that memorable day, she'd named him Charlie. Little Charlie.

Trace had a greenhouse installed within view of Hannah's kitchen window. Along with the greenhouse came seven plants of basil, lavender, peppermint, thyme, marjoram, lemongrass, and wintergreen. Seven bottles each for immediate use. For the next seven days and seven nights, Hannah and Trace stayed at the ranch enjoying the divine aromas diffused by the fragrant plants and oils.

They rested well, loved blissfully, and watched their garden grow. The Lucky 7 Ranch was back in business.

EPILOGUE

Trace and Hannah's love for each other grew too. They found time to work and play together almost every day. Oatie carried out his top-dog responsibilities seriously showing the puppy, Little Charlie, the ropes of life on a ranch. Word spread quickly through the small town of Stillwater that Hannah would never sell her cows for slaughter. Buttercup and the others would live to be contented old cows in the pastures at the Lucky 7. If the locals called her "the lady with the pet cows," so be it. She could live with that.

Trace added oats to the horses' buckets while Hannah fed the hens. Her thoughts returned to a delicate question she'd wanted to ask for several weeks. Today was the day.

"Once, you mentioned the existence of an older

brother. I've never seen him, and you never talk about him. How come? Where does he live? What does he do?" Hannah, in awe of the existence of *family,* waited anxiously to hear about the brother, her future brother-in-law.

"He's got a ranch in Montana." Trace never looked up and continued filling the buckets. Apparently, that was all he had to say on the subject of his brother. She'd let his unsatisfactory answer go for now, but not for long.

Hannah insisted on checking her cows every day, so side-by-side, they walked to the lower pasture; the dogs bounded ahead. "How long has it been since you saw your brother? And what's his name? I don't even know that."

"You're not going to let this go, are you?"

"No, of course not."

Trace removed his hat and ran his fingers through his hair. "Okay. His name is Troy. I've never found the time for a trip to Montana. I barely had the time to take care of the Lucky 7 properly." Under his breath, he mumbled, "And I've never been invited."

Though they walked in silence, questions tossed and tumbled within Hannah's brain. Did a family feud exist? A clash of male egos? Was Troy the black sheep of the McAllister clan? Her spirited imagination paralyzed her body. Standing perfectly still, her hands on her hips, she said, "*I'm* here now, and I'll take good care of the ranch. I suggest that you be the one to take the high road and fly up for a quick visit, a long weekend. What harm could come from that?"

"For years, I've known I should get up there and at least check out his property, but I don't want to leave you. I won't leave you, not now."

She refused to be his current excuse for not seeing his brother.

"I'll be fine," Hannah said, nodding her head with guarded confidence. "I have the greenhouse plants to care for, drawings to draw, and paintings to paint." With a wink and a grin, she added some motivation for his travel. "Without my handsome cowboy distracting me, the brushes will spend more time on the canvas, the pencils on the paper – well, you get the idea. And during your absence, my desire for you will build and deepen and . . ."

"I get it. You're very persuasive, Miss Hudson."

Was she persuading Trace to visit his brother? Or convincing herself she was not afraid to be alone? Either way, Hannah continued down this path as if she hadn't heard his concern. "Take a camera. I want pictures. Shoot everything. You must go, Trace. He's family. Go for a visit, check out his ranch and then, next time, take me with you." Then her eyes sparkled, her jaw dropped as a new idea came to mind. "You could surprise him. Just show up. Wouldn't that be fun?"

Trace grinned or was that a grimace? "Hannah, darlin', you've given me plenty to think about."

THEIR LOVE for each other was shatterproof, though their emotional and physical wounds remained disturbing and raw. The trauma they'd shared would linger for a while. Knowing there'd be difficult times ahead, they prayed for the day their near-death experience would dissolve into a distant, endurable memory.

In the meantime, Trace and Hannah wore brave faces and pretended a brief separation was no big deal. But, honestly, it was. Still, Hannah's words played over and over in Trace's head. JUST SHOW UP!

End of Book 1

In The McAllister Brothers Series

Author's Note

Sitting at my desk (handmade by my husband) in our log cabin high in the Colorado mountains, I stared out at the vast beauty before me. Surrounded by National Forest land and a few private ranches, the inspiration in every direction was almost overwhelming. However, I knew my next book would be about a ranch family. The details didn't come quite that quickly.

I experienced my first cattle drive up close and personal while moving slowly, carefully in my tiny Miata with the top down through about 300 bellowing cows and calves. I was eye-to-eye with the calves. The view of the huge cows was a blur of brown fur. Thrilling, to say the least. My car was never quite the same, but I developed a fondness for cattle. I shared that fondness with Hannah, **Colorado Takedown's** female protagonist.

I recall laughing when I heard myself say: "We need to make a trip to town for supplies." Supplies? Never said that when I lived in Tucson. After learning the hard way (more than once), we created a shopping list before heading out to avoid forgetting some essential items– toothpaste, matches, wine, TP. Just the drive to town and back took two hours. Nope. We didn't dare forget anything—especially not the list.

Then there was Oatie, the red-speckled cattle dog in this story. I modeled him after my real-life dog, Charlie. They were similar in so many ways. When I thought this novel was complete and ready to be uploaded to my editor, my dog Charlie died a tragic death. I felt the need to rewrite the ending of this story, which I did, though it was diffi- cult to do as a river of tears obscured the words as I tapped the keys on my laptop. If you've ever lost a beloved dog, you understand how I felt. Alas, another story for another time.

I hope you enjoyed Trace's story. If so, head on over and give Book 2 a try. There, a cowboy's gift of gab draws unthinkable danger to the love of his life and his unique Montana ranch. Read about love in a loft, an intense search and rescue, and life on a dude ranch in MONTANA COUNTDOWN.

Cricket

What's Next?

MONTANA COUNTDOWN
Book 2 in The McAllister Brothers Series
Troy, a wealthy rancher and Ivy, a beautiful, would-be novelist team up to save the ranch from unthinkable evil and end up fighting for their lives. It seemed the end was near when an unexpected visitor shocked them all.

WYOMING SUNDOWN
Book 3 in The McAllister Brothers Series
Trace and Troy agree to take their dad's challenge and ride horseback across the remote wastelands of Wyoming with Christmas just weeks away. Three men in danger, three women worry. What could possibly go wrong?

THANK YOU!

Thank you for reading *Colorado Takedown*.
Would you like to know when the next book in the
McAllister Brothers series is available? That's easy. Sign
up for Cricket's (almost) monthly NEWSLETTER and
you'll receive notifications of new books, giveaways, and
other exclusive content.

If you enjoyed this story, please leave a REVIEW
on Goodreads, Bookbub, or your favorite online retailer.
Reviews are helpful to readers and appreciated by
authors.

ABOUT THE AUTHOR

Cricket Rohman grew up in Estes Park, Colorado and spent her formative years among deer, coyotes, and fields of beautiful blue columbine. After retiring from a career in education, she became a full-time author writing contemporary fiction and western series and sagas about teachers, cowboys, dogs, lovers, and creative women inventing unique careers—just to mention a few.

Cricket loves to hear from readers.
Connect with her via:

Website http://www.cricketrohman.org
Facebook https://facebook.com/CricketRohmanAuthor
Twitter https://twitter.com/CricketRohman
Bookbub https://www.bookbub.com/authors/cricket-rohman
Email cricketrohman@gmail.com

MORE BOOKS BY CRICKET ROHMAN

You will find the links & excerpts for all of Cricket Rohman's books at

www.cricketrohman.org

The McAllister Brothers Series

Romantic Western Adventures

COLORADO TAKEDOWN, Book 1

This twisty cowboy adventure includes treachery, new love, family, courage, and amazing ranch animals.

MONTANA COUNTDOWN, Book 2

A wealthy rancher's story-telling tendency entices two eavesdroppers—a greedy criminal and a would-be novelist—to venture to his Montana ranch to search for his hidden treasure.

WYOMING SUNDOWN, Book 3

Clint McAllister's challenge put his sons in grave danger. Alice is furious about his foolish plan. It was almost Christmas, a bad time for such nonsense.

The Creative Hearts Sweet Romance Series

Creative Women Standalone Novellas

PHOEBE'S PHOTO FETISH

Phoebe Foxglove had three loves: Photography, Flowers, and Bobby. Two out of the three served her well.

ANNA'S ANIMAL HOUSE

Anna's new life began the moment she caught a glimpse of the flashing red light. There was no turning back now. But what was up ahead?

CAITLIN'S COW WASH

Caitlin feels trapped and out of place living in an old-fashion *Leave It To Beaver* household. Then, a perfect, win-win solution comes along—a cowboy named Cooper.

TINA'S TASTY TOURS

Tina has an impossible dream that comes with a substantial price tag. In the meantime, she works at the Punk Patio and a 1960s diner where she is required to look like Marilyn Monroe.

The Lindsey Lark Series

Fiction with Elements of Romance & Mystery

WANTED: AN HONEST MAN

Lindsey, a kinder teacher in survival mode after an unthinkable divorce, is brilliant in the classroom. Unfortunately, unwanted sinister challenges invade her off-hours.

LETTERS, LOVERS, & LIES

Jake and Lindsey are in love, but so much stands in their way. Fortunately, they are smart, multi-talented, and they love to laugh. Wendell, the 180-pound mastiff, is featured throughout this series.

HIT THE ROAD, JAKE!

Thrilling, romantic, and sprinkled with humor, this novel reinvents the 'buddy movie' concept with the written word … and a pretty woman. As Jake and Lindsey travel from Tucson to Estes Park in their RV, the dangers they face become deadly.

The Fantasy Maker Series

Contemporary Adventures

FOREVER ISLAND

JD won a contest and ended up on a deserted island somewhere in Micronesia. This is a wild beach adventure complete with danger, love, and a dog named Noodles.

WINTER'S BLUSH

The Fantasy Maker strikes an agreement with Clay. What's the catch? He must pretend to be someone he's not. A quick read that includes mountain hiking, rescue dogs, danger, and yes, some romance.

Saving Madeline

Standalone Contemporary Fiction

An entertaining story with humor, emotion, and an unusual mother-daughter relationship.

Christmas in the North Woods

A Children's Picture Book

Oliver Owl introduces the reader to his forest friends who are busy rehearsing for the annual Christmas Song Contest.